They stoo _____ is, staring at the city across the bay. Her silent comfort wrapped itself around him. Warmed the chill he felt inside. Made him feel whole again, if only for as long as they stood there together in silence.

"Well, I'd better go." She turned to him finally, slipping her hand from his. "But thank you for the coffee and the tour of your lovely home."

"The pleasure was mine." Jordan shoved his hands into his pockets. "Thank you for the ride and the chat."

There was something in her eyes as they met his. She opened her mouth to say something, then shut it quickly, dropping her gaze.

"Sasha, what is it?"

He should let it go. She'd decided against saying it. He should just leave it at that. But he couldn't. He needed to know.

She inhaled a deep breath, as if gathering her nerve. When her eyes met his, she leaned in, flattened her palms against his chest and rose on her toes to kiss him.

Dear Reader,

When my son was young, he took weekly art classes at the Cleveland Museum of Art. During his class, I roamed the museum, enchanted by its art and history. Sculpture was among my favorite mediums. So I was thrilled that Jordan Jace—the hero of *Seduced in San Diego*—is a sculptor.

Writing Jordan and Sasha's story allowed me to immerse myself in the fascinating world of sculpture, as I hadn't since I was a regular at the museum.

On the surface, Jordan seems skin-deep. But peel back the layers of this complex character, and you'll discover a big heart and the secrets weighing on it.

*Seduced in San Diego* is a fun, glamorous, sexy and emotional ride as Jordan and Sasha find their way to each other.

For series news, reader giveaways and more, join my VIP readers list at reeseryan.com.

Happy reading,

*Reese Ryan*

# SEDUCED
## IN
### San Diego

## REESE RYAN

**H** **HARLEQUIN**® KIMANI™ ROMANCE

Special thanks and acknowledgment
are given to Reese Ryan for her contribution to the
Millionaire Moguls of San Diego miniseries.

Recycling programs
for this product may
not exist in your area.

ISBN-13: 978-1-335-21663-2

Seduced in San Diego

Copyright © 2018 by Harlequin Books S.A.

**H** HARLEQUIN®
™ www.Harlequin.com

**Printed in U.S.A.**

**Reese Ryan** writes sinfully sweet romance. She challenges her characters with family and career drama and life-changing secrets while treating readers to an emotional love story filled with unexpected twists.

Past president of her local Romance Writers of America chapter and a panelist at the 2017 Los Angeles Times Festival of Books, Reese is an advocate of the romance genre and diversity in fiction.

Born and raised in the Midwest, Reese has lived in the South for nearly a decade and has an accent that confuses folks from both regions. Reese is an avid reader, a music lover and a musical soundtrack addict.

Connect with Reese via Instagram, Facebook or at reeseryan.com.

### Books by Reese Ryan

### Harlequin Kimani Romance

*Playing with Desire*
*Playing with Temptation*
*Playing with Seduction*
*Never Christmas Without You* (with Nana Malone)
*Seduced in San Diego*

Dedicated to all of the remarkable readers I've met during my publishing journey. You support African American and multicultural romance with your hard-earned dollars, valuable time, honest reviews and enthusiastic word of mouth. We are nothing without you.

## Acknowledgments

Shannon Criss and Keyla Hernandez, it has truly been a pleasure to work with you both. Thank you for your confidence in me, your patience and your enthusiastic support of my career, which has opened the door to additional opportunities within Harlequin.

Thank you to the Kimani editors, copywriters, cover artists and marketing team for your support. It has been an honor to be counted among the ranks of the remarkable Kimani Romance authors I have long admired.

# Chapter 1

Jordan Jace made a hard turn into the car park of the Prescott George headquarters. He got out, slamming the door of his black Karma Revero. Jordan glared at the stone-and-brick building.

He didn't appreciate being summoned to HQ. Vaughn Ellicott may have been a lieutenant when he served in the navy. But as a civilian, Vaughn was the treasurer of the San Diego chapter of Prescott George, not his commanding officer.

Jordan had joined Prescott George, or the Millionaire Moguls, as they were more commonly known, as a concession to his parents. He was the outlier in a family of wealthy London bankers who also had financial interests here in San Diego. His membership in the Millionaire Moguls was his way of throwing them a bone so they'd let go of their hopes that he'd eventually join the family business.

Jordan caught a glimpse of himself in the glass as he approached the building. Overpriced, tattered jeans. A T-shirt that read Icon. An unbuttoned, blue check shirt. Black motorcycle boots. His thick, curly hair grown out in twists.

He was no bloody banker. Artist. Metal sculptor. Professional badass. Any of the above applied. But a banker?

*Not in this lifetime or the next.*

Jordan checked his watch. It was nearly one o'clock in the afternoon. The opening for the latest exhibit of his work at his art gallery, Sorella, began in six hours.

*Vaughn better make this quick.*

Jordan scanned the modern, industrial space. Exposed brick. Concrete floors. Metal railings. Offices with glass walls and doors. Masculine, minimalist, modern furniture. No one was milling about the club.

He entered the building and made his way to the treasurer's office. There was Vaughn seated behind his glass-and-steel desk.

A career military man, Vaughn carried himself with poise. Stern scowl, confident demeanor, erect posture. But the man fidgeting behind that desk looked as if his seat was littered with thumbtacks, and he couldn't quite get comfortable.

*Something is very wrong.*

Whatever it was, Jordan didn't like it. Nor did he have the time or inclination to deal with any Millionaire Moguls drama today.

His assistant had been ringing his mobile all morning about the opening at the gallery that night. If he didn't get there soon, Lydia Dyson might need to crank up the dosage on her anxiety meds.

Jordan barged through Vaughn's partially open office door without knocking. He dropped onto one of the leather guest chairs on the other side of the man's desk and crossed one ankle over his knee.

"So, what is it you needed to see me about so bloody desperately that it couldn't wait until after my show tonight?" Jordan studied the man's reaction.

Vaughn's face went through a rapid series of emotions. Miffed that Jordan hadn't knocked. Unnerved about whatever it was he wanted to discuss. Annoyed with Jordan's cockiness after he read his T-shirt.

All of which deepened Jordan's smirk.

Vaughn returned his gaze to the paperwork he was reviewing on his desk.

"How long have you been a member of the San Diego chapter of Prescott George, Jordan?"

"Since I hopped across the pond. About a year ago, I guess."

"And how long were you a member of the London chapter before that?"

"A few years, I suppose. Why does it matter?" Jordan leaned into two fingers, pressed against his temple. "You didn't bring me down here to complete inconsequential paperwork that could have been handled just as easily via text, did you?"

"No." Vaughn put down his pen and frowned deeply, his hands steepled over his belly. "But I need to know how you feel about Prescott George."

*Something most definitely isn't right.*

Jordan sat up, clasping his hands in his lap. "Prescott George is a storied organization steeped in history. And over the years it's done a lot of good."

*There.*

He'd told the truth, but just enough of it that he wouldn't piss anyone off with what he really thought of the idea of an exclusive club for a bunch of wankers who thought themselves better than everyone else.

"But…?" Vaughn wasn't prepared to accept his textbook response. And he knew enough of Jordan to realize that if he poked a little harder he'd get the unfiltered truth.

"Why is this important? And why is it important now?" Jordan fidgeted in his chair, wired by the energy required to filter his thoughts and restrain his tongue.

Neither of which he was very good at.

"Because. I need to know." Vaughn narrowed his gaze, his jaw set.

"Fine. You want to know the truth? Then I'll tell you. Prescott George does quite a lot of good for its members and the community, but I happen to strongly disagree with its elitist, exclusionary nature."

"We can't all be principled artists with the luxury of living off our trust funds, now can we?" Vaughn seethed. His words were a direct hit to Jordan's ego, and he knew it.

It was true. When Jordan had first left college, he'd been dependent on his trust fund. However, he'd quickly made a name for himself on the London art scene and had eventually come to San Diego, purchased a studio and started to grow his brand here.

He wasn't exactly a household name, yet. However, he had public art installations in various cities in the US and in Europe. And he certainly wasn't dependent on his family's money any longer.

"There are plenty of self-made men like Chris Marland here, too," Vaughn continued, referring to the San Diego chapter president.

"And I admire such men." Jordan forced a smile. He refused to give Vaughn the satisfaction of knowing how peeved he was by his dig about him being a trust fund baby. "But we also have a great many members whose primary reason for joining the club is to enjoy the orgasmic pleasure of having someone else stroke their egos for a change." Jordan's smirk deepened when Vaughn scowled at his crude reference.

"Then why join the club at all?"

"Us nonconforming, trust fund babies must find some way to keep the parents happy, now mustn't we?" Jordan checked his watch again and frowned. He put both feet on the floor and clasped his hands between his knees. "Now, are you going to tell me what this is all about or not? I'm in no mood for a guessing game today, mate. Out with it already."

Vaughn cleared his throat and tipped his chin, his eyes meeting Jordan's. "Got the initial report on the recent break-in here."

"All right." Jordan leaned forward. "What've you learned about the robbery?"

Vaughn released a long sigh as he reviewed the document again. "There was evidence of a residue left behind, quite possibly by the perpetrator."

"What *kind* of residue?" Jordan was losing patience with Vaughn's deliberate evasiveness.

He met Jordan's gaze. "It was a powder often used in metalworking. The kind of thing a metal sculptor might use."

It took a few moments for Jordan to get his meaning. Not because he was daft, but because he was gobsmacked that the man could even think of making such an accusation.

"You can't possibly be accusing me of having anything to do with such a pedestrian prank? No, you must surely be having a laugh at my expense." Jordan shot to his feet. "Any other day, perhaps I'd find it amusing. But today I've got no time for joking, mate. Got an exhibition at the gallery tonight, or have you forgotten?"

"I'm afraid it's no joke." Vaughn looked pained by the entire ordeal.

"You're mad as a bag of ferrets if you believe this bollocks." Jordan paced the floor. He gestured around the office. "Nothing here is worth my time. If I wanted it, I'd simply purchase it for myself."

"Since you have such a love-hate relationship with the club, perhaps you did it as a joke. Or maybe as a way to piss everyone here off."

"Do I look the sort of tosser that would risk getting nicked for a practical joke?"

"Then how do you explain the metalworking powder residue found at the scene?" Vaughn kept his voice calm. Controlled. Rather than settling him, it only made him want to punch the man in his smug face.

"That's not my job, now is it?" Jordan folded his arms defiantly, then blew an exasperated breath as he flopped into the chair again. "Innocent until proven guilty and all that."

"True." Vaughn nodded sagely, tapping a pen on the blasted investigative report. He raised his eyes to meet Jordan's again. "But then there's the anonymous reports received by a local gossip blog."

"Naming me as the culprit?"

"Hinting that the heist was an inside job." Vaughn put the pen down and studied his reaction. "Put the residue and the news that it's an inside job together and—"

"You and the wanker who set you on to this idea are completely barmy. So what if there was residue from my metalworking? I'm in here often enough, aren't I?"

"I agree that you're not a very likely suspect. You may be a pompous ass, but I doubt that you're a thief." Vaughn seemed relieved. "Still, I had to ask."

"I understand." Jordan hadn't realized his heart was racing. His breathing slowed and he nodded. "So who do you suspect?"

"That's just it." Vaughn shrugged. "I don't have any idea why someone inside our club would do this. Especially now…when we've been nominated as Prescott George's Chapter of the Year. The timing couldn't be worse."

"True. That still puts us no closer to knowing exactly who the dodgy prat is who'd do something like this."

"I just printed out a few copies of our membership list." Vaughn shoved some papers across his desk at Jordan. "Got a few minutes to go over it with me? I'd love a second opinion on who might be responsible."

Jordan groaned and checked his Devon Tread watch. He honestly didn't have time for this tosh.

But perhaps he should show some gratitude for Vaughn's confidence in him.

He picked up the stack of names and pored over them. After a half an hour of comparing notes on various members of the club, Jordan's phone rang again. This time it was his father. His mother had rang a handful of times earlier in the day.

Jordan sent the call to voice mail. He didn't want to hear either of their excuses about why they wouldn't be able to make tonight's exhibition this time.

"This round of who's the barmy bastard has been fun." Jordan shoved his phone back into his pocket and stood. "But I've got a show to put on tonight. Shall I expect you and your lovely wife to be in attendance?"

"Miranda and I have a previous engagement tonight. I'm sorry we'll miss it." Vaughn settled back in his seat. "And I hope there are no hard feelings about our conversation today."

"You didn't have much of a choice, I s'pose." Jordan shrugged. "But I can't promise to be so forgiving if it should ever happen again."

Jordan put on his shades and made his way back to his car. Time to focus on tonight's event. The only thing he really cared about.

# Chapter 2

Sasha Charles read the invitation to the Jordan Jace exhibition at his gallery, Sorella, for the third time. She scanned the website for the gallery and studied his handsome face.

Smooth brown skin. Intense, mesmerizing eyes. A brilliant, mischievous smile. There was something about the man that made her want to know more about him. Then there was his art. Public installations that stood several stories high against the San Diego skyline.

Powerful. Intriguing. Enigmatic.

Much like the man himself from what she'd been able to gather.

Sasha walked through her closet in search of the perfect dress. Something that was all business, but would still capture Jordan Jace's eye when she walked into his gallery.

She lifted a dress custom made for her by one of her clients—a local fashion designer.

Sasha had been waiting for the right occasion to wear the dress. The navy, off-shoulder dress had a mermaid silhouette. The top was made of lace and there was a lace detail on the train.

Sasha held the dress against her and nodded. A sly smile curved the corner of her mouth.

*Absolutely perfect. Jordan Jace won't know what hit him.*

Sasha laid the dress out on her bed, kicked off her shoes and got ready for the night ahead.

Jordan stood on the second level of his art gallery and surveyed the space. Tried to see it as a first-time visitor or potential client would.

He loved everything about Sorella. From its name to the raw elements that comprised the site. Exposed brick walls. Restored original wood floors. An open loft and staircase constructed of black steel.

The spare feel of the showroom allowed the art to be the real star. The paintings of some of San Diego's best upcoming artists adorned the walls of the gallery. Sculptures cast in bronze, copper, steel, marble and clay anchored the space. And today a variety of his pieces took center stage on both levels.

Jordan worked with found elements of metal and reclaimed wood to create works of art that were truly unique. Pieces each viewer interpreted differently.

It was an honor to have public art installations in San Diego and the UK. To share his art with an entire community. Yet, there was something truly intimate about a buyer falling in love with one of his sculptures and making it part of their home or office.

It was a tremendous feeling his parents would never understand. Not that they'd ever tried. Instead, they'd treated his art as if it were a teenage indulgence. Something he needed to work out of his system before he finally gave it up and took a "real" job in their family business.

"How does everything look?" Lydia shoved her glasses up the bridge of her nose as she stood beside him.

"Brilliant. You've done a bang-up job, Lydia." Arms still folded, he glanced at the woman quickly, then returned to surveying the gallery for any missed details.

"Is there anything I've forgotten?" She stood ready with a notebook and pen.

"Is the bar completely stocked?"

Guests would be offered complimentary champagne and hors d'oeuvres. But they could order any-thing they desired from the bar anchoring the center of the room.

"Yes. They have all of the top-shelf spirits you requested."

"Did we get that wine in from—"

"The wineries you visited in Baja last month during the Prescott George tour?" Lydia finished his thought. "Yes."

"Very good. Has the caterer arrived yet?"

"She's setting up now."

"You're remarkable, as always." Jordan turned to face the woman. Lydia's title was assistant, but truthfully, she did it all. She handled paperwork, managed the gallery, assisted with the curation of artwork and generally kept him on track. All with-out complaint. "And you look smashing tonight. As always," he added with a broad smile that made her blue eyes twinkle.

Per his parents' voice mails and text messages filled with excuses, neither of them would be in at-tendance tonight, though they were both in town. But an impressive list of wealthy and well-known residents of San Diego would be on hand. Along with a few out-of-towners who'd flown in just for the event.

Tonight would be memorable—regardless of whether his parents deemed the event worthy of their presence.

* * *

Jordan flashed his biggest smile for a wealthy patron who'd bought several of his sculptures for her homes in London and Los Angeles. Vivian Avery had been the first person to purchase a major piece from him who hadn't been connected to or referred by a member of his family or Prescott George. Ten years later, she was still one of his most ardent supporters.

Tonight the older woman was in the market for a smaller scale piece right for her lavish New York apartment.

Jordan chatted with a few other patrons milling about the gallery. He talked with two other gallery owners who'd been pressing him to collaborate on a local arts festival. They hoped the project would bring a wider range of visitors to all three galleries. Jordan wasn't willing to commit on the project just yet. But he was personable and showed just enough interest to keep the two other gallery owners' hopes alive.

"Phenomenal event, Jordan." His eldest brother, Marlon, exchanged his empty champagne glass for a filled one floating by on a server's tray.

His brothers Michael and Joseph heartily agreed.

"Thank you for coming tonight. All of you, but you especially." Jordan indicated his brother Marlon who'd arranged a business meeting in San Diego for the sole purpose of attending his event. "I know you have to be off soon to catch your red-eye flight back home."

"Since he's flying the private jet, Michael and I are tagging along." Joseph nibbled on pâté on crostini. "We'll be back here in a week or two."

Jordan gave his brothers a quick hug. "I really do appreciate you being here."

"Mum and Dad really did want to be here," Marlon said quickly. "They've been trying to ring you all day to tell you as much themselves."

"You shouldn't brush them off that way. If for no other reason than they keep ringing the three of us all day. As if that will force you to answer your mobile."

"I love them, but I've heard all of their excuses before." Jordan winced, his lips pressed into a hard line. "Wasn't much up for such utter tosh today. Had my fill of it for the day over at the Prescott George office."

"What happened?" Michael crooked his brow.

"Nothing worth discussing," Jordan said quickly. "And nothing for any of you to worry about." He caught a glimpse of Lydia waving him over. "If I don't see you before you leave, have a safe flight."

Jordan answered a few questions Lydia asked on behalf of a client inquiring about a custom piece. He stopped to talk to the bartenders, then mingled with a few other guests. Then he noticed…*her*.

He watched the woman in a long, navy dress that

hugged her lush curves. The dress was incredibly sexy without being too revealing. A line she trod remarkably well. Her movements were so smooth and fluid she seemed to float across the room.

Jordan's attention was drawn to the smooth skin of her back and shoulders. Trailed up her long, elegant neck. He usually fancied women with long hair. Enamored with the thought of winding it round his fist. But the woman's hair was cut into a short, pixie style that perfectly suited her impish smile.

A smile that indicated she knew something the rest of the world didn't. A secret he suddenly needed to know.

As the woman sipped her champagne, her head tipped back slightly. Jordan found himself studying her throat. Her jawline. Her delicate cheekbones.

She walked around the sculpture she'd been assessing for the past few minutes, giving him an excellent view of her face.

*Even better.*

The woman was beyond fit. Even beyond stunning. Gorgeous, delicate facial features. Warm brown skin that practically glowed. Long, lean limbs.

Just cataloging her many fine attributes sent a shiver down his spine.

And she appeared to be without a companion for the evening. A dilemma he would most happily remedy.

Jordan wandered beside the woman and stared

at the sculpture in silence for a moment. He sipped his champagne, then turned to her. "What do you think of it?"

"Me?" She gave him only a cursory glance, then returned her attention to the piece.

"You seemed to be making quite a study of it." He shifted his gaze back to the piece. "Surely you've come to some conclusion."

They stood silently in front of the sculpture. Two long, curved sheets of weathered steel shielded shiny steel cylinders. Hammered ribbons of steel circled the outside of the structure and appeared to float around it.

"The cylinders inside represent the status quo. The curved sheets of steel represent the artist." She stepped forward, pointing to each section. "He desperately wants to break away from the status quo. To turn it on its ear. The floating ribbons of steel represent the possibilities that are out there, if only he can break free of limiting, status quo expectations."

The woman turned to him. Her eyes locked with his. Slowly, her impish grin turned into a full-blown smirk. She broke into melodic laughter, her eyes twinkling.

"I'm kidding." She drank more of her champagne as she turned back to study the piece again. "I have no idea what it means. All I know is that I really like it."

A wide smile tightened Jordan's cheeks.

*Beautiful. A sense of humor. And she doesn't take herself too seriously.*

Jordan would be well on his way to falling in love with this woman, if he weren't completely opposed to the notion of love at first sight. Or love in general. At least at this stage of his life.

Didn't mean they couldn't have a bit of fun together, if she was up for it.

"Well, it can be yours for the bargain price of one hundred and twenty-five thousand dollars." He extended a hand to her. "I'm Jordan Jace, the artist. And I desperately do want to break out of the limiting status quo."

"Sasha Charles." She placed her warm hand in his much larger one. "Pleasure to meet you, Mr. Jace."

"No, Ms. Charles, the pleasure is all mine, I assure you." He held her hand in his a beat or two longer than was customary. His smile widened when she didn't pull her hand away. He reluctantly released her hand. "And call me Jordan. I insist."

"Only if you call me Sasha." Her smile lit her eyes. She finished her champagne, then placed the empty glass on a passing tray.

"One moment, please." He halted the server, then turned to her. "Shall I grab another for you?"

"Why, are you one of those artists whose work is better interpreted the more you've had to drink?"

A deep, belly laugh erupted from him that turned

the heads of several people in attendance. She joined in on the laughter.

"Not particularly," he managed finally. "But according to my family, they find me far less puzzling once they've had a drink or two."

"Then maybe I should have another." Sasha took a glass of champagne from the server's tray and thanked him. "Just in case."

Jordan definitely liked this woman.

"So, Miss… Sasha, do you often attend gallery openings?" He fell in line beside her as she moved to another piece.

"Sadly, no. I appreciate art, but I'm not much of an aficionado. I simply know what I like when I see it." She took another sip, her gaze meeting his.

"Then to what do I owe the honor of your attendance here tonight?"

"I was invited to attend tonight's event." She walked around the smaller sculpture, her eyes meeting his again, briefly, before returning to the piece. "By a member of Prescott George."

"I see."

If he had to be a member of the club, it might as well pay dividends. And if he had his membership in the Millionaire Moguls to thank for bringing this stunning woman into his gallery, well, then maybe membership in the club was worthwhile, after all.

"Which member should I thank for extending the

invitation to you? And what prompted you to accept it?" He watched her reaction as she assessed the piece.

"I'm sorry to interrupt, Jordan." Lydia approached hurriedly, pushing her eyeglasses up the bridge of her nose. She clutched her ever-present notepad. "But Mrs. Avery wants to buy three of your pieces—including *Opposing Forces*." She nodded toward the sculpture they'd just left. The centerpiece of the exhibition. "But she has a couple of questions she'd like to ask you first."

"Last chance." He winked at Sasha, who laughed, before he turned back to Lydia. "Please tell Mrs. Avery that I'll be with her in just a moment."

Jordan returned his attention to Sasha. "Seems you're my good luck charm. I didn't expect that *Opposing Forces* would move tonight."

"Does that mean I'm entitled to a cut of the sale?" Sasha pursed her pouty, pink lips, a smile teasing the edges of her mouth.

"We'll see." He smiled. "I have to go, but I won't be very long. I hope you're still around when I'm done. There are a few more pieces I'd love to hear your opinion of."

"Take your time." Sasha's gaze held his. "I wouldn't think of going anywhere."

## Chapter 3

Jordan Jace's photos hadn't done him justice. The man was absolutely gorgeous. His brilliant smile demanded attention from halfway across the room. And there was something truly magical about his laugh and the touch of his hand.

His penetrating gaze had sent shivers down her spine. And his mouth. There was something about his full lips that made hers burn with the desire to taste them.

It was official. The slight crush she'd developed on Jordan Jace as she'd studied him was now full-blown infatuation.

Her hand curled into a fist at her side, remembering how his large hand had engulfed hers. The tingling in her palm when her skin had touched his. And the trail of electricity that had skittered down her spine and into places she'd rather not admit.

No wonder Jordan had developed a reputation as a playboy during his short time in San Diego. She'd watched as the art groupies and wealthy patrons—like Vivian Avery, a beauty product heiress—had fawned all over him.

Sasha wouldn't have been surprised if the wealthy heiress had purchased that piece just to bring Jordan back to her side and away from Sasha.

It was just as well. She could use a moment of distance. An opportunity to get her head back on straight. She hadn't come here to let Jordan Jace sweep her off her feet. Her job was to ensure that he understood exactly why he needed her.

Having had a taste of the challenge ahead, she had no intention of leaving the gallery without doing just that.

Sasha checked her watch. Jordan had been gone for more than an hour. His business with Vivian Avery hadn't seemed to take very long. However, he'd been pulled into a conversation every time he'd headed in her direction again.

Jordan Jace was quickly becoming a star in the San Diego art world. He was doing exactly as he should. Courting patrons and potential buyers.

So why did she feel a desperate sense of longing as Jordan moved from one person to the next? And the tug of the green-eyed monster as he flashed that big smile and focused his penetrating gaze on the other women there?

*This is business, not* The Dating Game. *Stay focused and stop acting like a jealous girlfriend.*

Sasha heaved a sigh and passed on another glass of champagne. She checked her watch one last time.

She'd come here tonight to observe Jordan. She hadn't intended to engage him in conversation. Not yet, anyway. He was busy tonight. It would be better if she made an appointment to meet with him in his office. In a situation that felt a lot less…flirtatious.

Sasha grabbed a brochure and headed toward the exit.

"You're not leaving." Jordan caught her elbow before she reached the door. "I know I've been away a lot longer than I expected, but I'd love it if you'd stay a bit longer."

"You're obviously quite busy tonight. Which is exactly what you want." She forced a smile to hide the disappointment she felt at leaving his company.

"If you stay, I'll make it worth your while." His eyes lit up as a smile slid across his handsome face. The kind of smile it was hard to say no to.

She leaned in closer, her voice low. "And exactly how do you plan to make it worth my while?"

"With a private tour." His intense gaze felt like a

laser peering into her soul. Dissolving her will like copper in a hot, smelting furnace.

"The gallery is quite lovely, but I do believe I've seen just about all of it during the course of the evening. Except, of course, the men's room."

Jordan's laughter rang through the gallery and her cheeks heated in response.

"I think it's better if that particular space remains a mystery. However, I'd love to give you a behind-the-scenes tour of the gallery, including my studio next door."

Sasha's pulse sped up, her chest rising and falling rapidly. She couldn't tear her gaze away from his.

*What is it about this man that is so...mesmerizing?*

Jordan Jace certainly wasn't the first handsome man with a great smile she'd encountered. So why was he so damn intriguing?

Perhaps too intriguing for someone she hoped to work with.

Saying yes to his flirtatious overture was a bad idea. And yet…she couldn't say no.

"I don't suppose I could turn down an opportunity like that." She stepped away to create some space. He released her arm with a knowing smile. "How exactly did I merit such a high honor?"

His eyes twinkled. "Because, Sasha Charles, there is something about you that I find inspiring. And I can't rest until I know exactly what that is."

Jordan was gone before she could respond.

Sasha exhaled, her eyes pressed closed momentarily. She'd hoped that Jordan's attraction to her would make her job easier. But her attraction to him would surely make the situation more challenging.

Still, this was an opportunity she couldn't pass up. So she'd have to put on her big-girl panties, keep Jordan Jace out of them and pull herself together.

"I'm sorry, ma'am, but the gallery is closed now." Jordan's assistant, a pretty woman with mousy brown hair, sparkling blue eyes and over-size glasses, approached Sasha.

She stood from the red sofa where she'd been seated. The glittery heels she'd chosen to wear were gorgeous, but her feet were killing her.

"I'm waiting. For Jordan." Sasha suddenly felt incredibly self-conscious. How many art groupies had sat in the same seat spouting the same line?

The woman frowned. "Did Jordan ask you to wait for him?" The question felt accusatory.

"Yes, I did." Jordan walked over to the woman and put a reassuring hand on her shoulder. "Sasha Charles is my guest this evening." He turned to Sasha. "Sasha, meet Lydia Dyson, my right hand here at the gallery. I honestly don't know what I'd do without her."

"Nice to meet you," the woman said, though her tone indicated otherwise. She squinted at Sasha as she pushed her glasses up the bridge of her nose. When her eyes met Jordan's briefly, she smiled. "He's being too kind, of course. I'm incredibly lucky that I get to work with the great Jordan Jace." Lydia gazed at him adoringly. A fact that seemed to go right over Jordan's head. "But I appreciate the compliment, anyway."

"I'll lock up tonight. You head on home. And come in a few hours late tomorrow. I insist," he added, before Lydia could object. Jordan broadened his smile. "Take a couple of bottles of champagne on your way out. You've earned them. Tonight was magnificent."

Lydia perked up and nodded. The woman turned and walked away, tossing a good-night over her shoulder.

"Hey." Jordan shoved his hands in his pockets, his eyes meeting hers with an intensity that sparked something inside her.

"Hey." Sasha tightened her grip on her clutch. Heat filled her cheeks.

"I'm glad you stayed." He indicated a doorway at the back of the studio and they both walked toward it. "Can I get you a glass of wine or a bite to eat?"

"I've had quite enough tonight already, thank you." Sasha held up a hand. There was no way she could pull off this encounter successfully if she wasn't completely sober. Not with electricity dancing up her spine as she walked beside this man.

"As you wish." He opened the door, which led down a narrow corridor.

Sasha halted in her tracks and took a deep breath. Her eyes met his. "Look, Jordan, I appreciate the chance to tour your studio. But if the invitation is really just the modern-day equivalent of offering to 'show me your etchings'…"

Jordan's deep belly laugh made her cheeks burn, but she couldn't help chuckling, too. He raised his hands, his palms facing her.

"I have every intention of being a gentleman tonight. I assure you." He grinned. "I just thought you might like to see the method behind my madness, so to speak. Of course, after tonight…well that, love, is up to you."

Sasha exhaled and headed down the brick corridor. Her heels clicked against the concrete floor as Jordan walked beside her.

Finally, he opened another door and turned on the light. The unfinished brick walls, stained concrete floor and steel beams overhead gave the cavernous space the same spare, raw feel as the gallery.

"My assistant hosed down the floor this morning, but it is still a working studio. So perhaps you should be careful with that lovely dress." Jordan held the door open.

"Lydia hosed down the floor?" Sasha gathered the hem of her dress in one hand and followed Jordan into the studio.

"No, Lydia is my gallery assistant," Jordan clarified. "A young man named Marcus Whitten is my studio assistant."

"I see." Sasha surveyed the space. It smelled of welded metal, but it was surprisingly clean for a studio that housed rolls of sheet metal and industrial shelving bearing metal pipes, buckets of nuts, bolts, chains and a variety of other cast-off pieces of metal. "And what does a sculptor's assistant do? Besides hose down the floor?"

"Thankfully, quite a bit." Jordan beckoned her farther into the space. "When I started out, I did everything myself. The salvaging, the cutting and prepping and all of the welding. Sometimes I worked on more than one piece at a time, but it could take weeks or even months to complete them."

"And now?"

"Now I have Marcus. Quite the promising sculptor in his own right. But for now, he helps me out with the grunt work around here. Frees me up to focus on the artistic bits."

"He's paying his dues, I suppose." Sasha strolled along the space with Jordan. Past heavy tools and stockpiles of salvaged metals and reclaimed wood.

"As did I."

"You? Doing grunt work?" Sasha stopped and turned to him, barely holding back an incredulous grin. "Why do I find that so difficult to believe?"

"Doesn't fit the millionaire playboy narrative, I

know." He chuckled. "But it's true. I studied studio art in university for a couple of years. University life and rules didn't quite agree with me. So I left."

"Now that, I can believe." Sasha tried not to allow herself to be drawn in by those glittering eyes and that infinite charm, enhanced by a very sexy British accent. It was a losing battle. "I doubt your parents were very happy with that decision."

"They weren't." For the first time, there was a flash of darkness in his expression. "I'm the black sheep in the Jace family. The sole artist in a family full of bankers. My mum and dad thought I'd gone mad when I left university and went to work as a studio assistant for a mere pittance. Truthfully, they still think me a bit bonkers."

Sasha's heart ached for Jordan. He behaved as if he was unconcerned about the opinions of others. Though clearly, he was wounded by his parents' rejection of his career choice.

The topic of his parents was a subject best avoided for as long as possible.

"Did you work for a sculptor?"

"Eventually." He stuffed his hands in his pockets, his confident smile fixed firmly in place again. "But first I was assistant to a painter and then a multi-media artist. Then I went to work for a remarkable sculptor who worked with clay."

"Your apprenticeships served you well. I can see the influence of all three mediums in your work."

Sasha turned her attention to an assemblage of scrap metal laid out on the floor. "Is this what you're working on now?"

"It is. Commissioned for a corporate office headquartered in LA." He gripped his chin, studying the metal fragments, as if seeing them for the first time.

Sasha walked carefully around the collection of metal scraps until she stood opposite him. When she looked up, he was no longer studying the metal pieces on the floor. He was studying her.

Electricity trailed down her spine and the room suddenly felt warm. She dropped her gaze to the assemblage of scraps arranged on the floor again.

"So a commissioned piece like this. How does it work? Does the client tell you what they want?"

"This isn't color by numbers, love." His smile widened. He was clearly amused by the very suggestion that he'd execute someone else's design. "I don't have anything against anyone who does work that way, mind you. It simply doesn't work for me. Black sheep who has an uneasy relationship with rules, remember?" He poked a thumb to his chest.

"Good point." She nodded sagely, her cheeks tightening in a smile. "So, what is your process? Do you sketch out your designs, then find the materials you need?"

"Only when an idea begins in my head. Perhaps I'm inspired by something I've seen, there's a concept I want to express or I have a persistent vision

I can't let go of." Jordan stooped, rearranging a few of the metal scraps. "Other times, I select salvaged pieces like these and play around with them. Try out different configurations until a design speaks to me."

Jordan scrutinized the pieces intently, and Sasha assessed him.

"So how did you come by your remarkable studio assistant Marcus?"

"I met him during a workshop I gave for local high school students." Jordan stood, dusting off his hands. He retrieved a clean rag from a nearby metal table and cleaned them. "Marcus was bright and incredibly talented. Eager to learn about art. But he was struggling with the rest of his schoolwork and he'd become a fixture in the headmaster's office."

"Then why'd you take a chance on him?"

Jordan shrugged, still focused on the configuration of items laid out on the concrete floor. "I see a little of myself in him, I suppose." He raised his gaze to hers, then laughed. "And that is why I don't normally tell people stories like this."

"Why? What did I do?"

"You've got that face…as if you've just seen a baby take its first steps or something."

"I do not."

"Yes, you do. And I don't work with kids like Marcus for recognition. Neither is it a wholly self-less act." He gestured toward another metal table where a smaller piece was taking shape. "The boy's got a good eye. And he's a very hard worker."

"Obviously." Sasha surveyed the piece. An assemblage of metal pipes and fittings were arranged in the shape of legs and feet. "But if he was already struggling with school...won't a demanding job make things worse?"

Jordan stuffed his hands in his pockets and assessed Sasha, as if debating whether he should tell her the rest.

"I pay him a decent hourly wage, but the rest goes toward a tutor. Like I said, he's quite bright. He just learns a bit differently."

"And he agreed to the deal?"

"He's never missed a tutoring session and his grades have improved dramatically." Jordan's eyes twinkled with pride. He indicated the various machines along one wall. "And he's learned to work all of the machinery here. Skills that would serve him well if he needed to go into a trade, for a time, at least."

"It's all a facade, isn't it?" Sasha couldn't help the smile that spread across her face or the fluttering in her chest.

"Sorry?" Jordan crooked a brow, puzzled.

"You behave as if you don't care about anything or anyone but your art, but you do. You care about the environment—that's why you use discarded wood and metal. You care about underprivileged youth—that's why you do the workshops. And you obviously care deeply about both of your assistants."

"I never purported to be a monster. And if you thought as much, I doubt you'd be here now."

"Actually... I have a very particular reason for being here." Sasha was reluctant to bring their lovely evening together to what would likely be an abrupt end.

"If the answer is anything other than you being taken with the art or the artist, I'll be terribly disappointed." He stuffed his hands in his pockets.

"You're a brilliant artist, Jordan. And far more fascinating than I would've suspected." Sasha's heart beat faster. She reached into her small clutch, pulled out a business card and handed it to him. "But the reason I came tonight is because I'm a brand strategist, and I'd love to work with you."

Jordan accepted the card and reviewed it. One eyebrow shifted upward. "I don't know if you've noticed, Ms. Charles, but tonight's event was packed. We cleared a half million dollars in sales and commissions tonight alone."

"Impressive indeed." Sasha nodded. "But I believe you're capable of even more. I can help you double or triple what you made tonight. More importantly, I'll work tirelessly to help raise your visibility internationally and smooth over some of the issues you've had in the past with bad press."

"And exactly how do you plan to do that, Ms.

Charles?" He'd reverted to formal address since they were talking business. Yet, there was unmistakable flirtatiousness in his tone.

"I can't give all my trade secrets away for free, now can I?" She smiled. "But I would begin by honing your online presence. Currently, your social media real estate is either absent or lacking the brilliance and creativity worthy of a true creative genius."

"I'm a creative genius, am I?"

"I don't think anyone at the gallery this evening would dispute that."

Jordan stepped closer, his heat enveloping her. "Including you?"

Sasha swallowed hard, her knees quivering slightly as she inhaled his delicious scent. "Me, especially."

"Sounds tempting." Jordan's heated gaze left Sasha unsure whether he was referring to her or her proposal. Surprisingly, the former was more tempting than the latter. "But I confess myself nostalgic for simpler times. When one needn't manage their brand or monitor their online presence. Life is too short to be consumed by the opinion of the faceless masses. Or even those much closer to home, for that matter."

"Times change, and this is the reality of doing business now," she stated firmly. "I know it seems like a hassle to manage your brand. But handled properly, it's the key to achieving everything you want."

"You presume to know what that is?" Jordan cocked a brow.

He was testing her.

"Yes." Sasha raised her chin. "Money and notoriety are important to you. That's obvious from the eye-catching cars and the occasional 'wild child' antics. But there's so much more to Jordan Jace than you let on."

Jordan folded his arms. "Such as?"

Sasha smiled, her confidence rising. "You use recycled and found materials in your work, and though you drive very pricey cars, they're all eco-friendly. So obviously caring for the environment is a huge issue for you."

"That one was easy." Jordan narrowed his gaze. "You'll have to do better than that to convince me."

"All right." Sasha nodded. If Jordan Jace needed convincing, she could handle that. "Your work with underprivileged kids is as important to you as bringing beauty into the world through your art." When he didn't reply, she indicated the table where Marcus's sculpture stood. "*This* is the legacy you want to leave, isn't it? A man who left the world, and the people in it, in a much better state than he found them."

Jordan rubbed his chin and cleared his throat.

She'd touched a nerve and it made him uncomfortable.

*Good.*

He had to be willing to get uncomfortable if they
were going to work together. Evidently, she'd have
to accept operating outside of her comfort zone, too.

"Well, Miss Charles, why don't you let me think
about your request and get back to you?" Jordan
headed for the door.

Panic spread through Sasha's chest. She'd pushed
him too hard. Now she needed to play the card she'd
been holding on to.

"You never did get an answer to your question."
She remained rooted in her spot, though her pulse
raced.

Jordan turned back to her. "About?"

"Which member of Prescott George invited me
here tonight?"

"No, I didn't, did I?" He folded his arms, one
brow raised. She'd gotten his attention. "Who do I
have to thank for the lovely sales pitch?"

Sasha inhaled deeply. Tried to keep her limbs
from trembling. "Jonathan Jace."

"My father invited you here? Why? He doesn't
give one whit whether or not the gallery is successful."

"I doubt that's true." She stepped closer, shrink-
ing the gap between them. "But your mother obviously does. She's the person who hired me."

"Exactly when did you plan to tell me all this?" Jordan scowled.

"When it became relevant." Sasha maintained his gaze and shrugged. "It just did."

"So this entire performance tonight was an elaborate ruse at my expense?"

"No, it was a test." She stepped even closer, forcing her gaze to meet his. "For both of us. I needed to know that you were someone I could work with. That your art and what you stand for are things I believe in. Without that foundation, there's no way I can sell your brand to the world."

"And what's the verdict?" He folded his arms and stared down his nose at her.

"I was already a fan of the art. But now I'm infinitely impressed with the artist." Sasha smiled, invoking his earlier statement.

Jordan shook his head and seemed to chuckle, in spite of himself. "Okay, Sasha." He put emphasis on the use of her given name again. "I'll make you a deal."

She folded her arms and tipped her chin upward. "Let's hear it."

"I'll listen to your proposal for expanding my brand…over dinner. My treat."

Sasha inhaled deeply. Tried not to let him see her blink or how her knees were trembling. She gripped her clutch tightly with both hands and exhaled slowly. "A working dinner?"

"If it makes you feel better to call it that."

"What would you call it?" The brooch on her silk clutch dug into her skin.

"A date, of course." Jordan chuckled in response to her opened mouth and widened eyes. His nostrils flared and a sexy-as-sin smirk curved one side of his sensuous mouth. "Careful, love. Now I can see you a bit more clearly."

"What do you mean?" Heat crawled up her spine and the space between them seemed to evaporate.

"You're Miss Prim and Proper. The one who can't bear the thought of breaking the rules." He walked around her, studying her as if she were a museum piece. He leaned in closer. His warm breath tickled her skin. His tone was teasing. "I doubt you've ever knowingly broken a single rule."

Heat filled her cheeks and a knot tightened in her belly. Yes, he was definitely testing her.

If Jordan Jace thought she'd be run off by a little teasing and a lot of flirtation, he had no idea whom he was dealing with. Unlike Jordan, Sasha hadn't come from money. But she knew how to play the game, and she wasn't easily intimidated. And dealing with a difficult client? That was just her average Tuesday.

Sasha lengthened her spine, her eyes meeting his. "Just tell me when and where."

## Chapter 4

Jordan pushed in Sasha's chair, then settled in the seat across from her. The woman was even more mesmerizing than he remembered. A remarkable feat, since he hadn't been able to get her face and memorable curves out of his head for the past three days.

Sasha Charles had been all he could think of. He'd even taken out his charcoal pencils and sketched the face and form that had kept him awake late at night. Tossing and turning with the desire to have her in his bed.

Tonight, he'd pulled out all the stops to impress her.

Secured reservations at the hottest French restaurant in town, despite their customary thirty-day waiting list. He'd insisted on picking her up in his Porsche Panamera Sport Turismo. And he'd placed their orders in perfect French.

Still, Sasha seemed unaffected. As if it were a run-of-the-mill Friday night.

She pulled out two black folders with gold lettering on them and handed him one. "You asked to see my plan for growing your brand? Well, here it is."

"You want to do this right now?" Jordan opened the folder emblazoned with the name of the marketing agency Sasha worked for.

"I appreciate the lovely gesture, of course. I've been wanting to try this place since they opened six months ago." Sasha glanced around the elegant restaurant. "However, I thought it best to establish the tone at the outset. Whatever you might call it, for me, this is very much a business dinner."

"Point taken." Jordan nodded sagely. "And maybe you're right. Best to get all of the business out of the way so we can move on to more…fun aspects of the evening."

Sasha's eyes widened and she blinked several times. "Jordan, I don't want to give you the wrong idea about tonight. I want to work with you, of course. But not if that means you expect me to—"

"Oh God, no." Jordan held his hands up. "I know that I made this dinner a requirement for me to consider working with you, but I'd never…" He couldn't even say the words. "That isn't even remotely my style. I assure you. However, I am quite taken with you, Sasha. I'd like to get to know you better. I don't see anything wrong with that, do you?"

Sasha sank her teeth into her luscious lower lip, the wheels turning in her lovely head. She didn't respond to his question. Instead, she took a sip of the mineral water she'd ordered instead of wine.

Finally, she raised her eyes to his. "In that case, I should tell you that you don't need to try so hard to impress me."

Jordan leaned forward. "And why is that?"

"I'm already impressed. You're a brilliant artist, Jordan. I know that your pieces will be in museums all over the world within five or ten years. Kids will be studying them in art classes in twenty."

Sasha paused as the server put their appetizers on the table. A warm puff pastry filled with Camembert cheese and served with a side of fruit chutney. She asked for her water glass to be refilled, repeating her insistence that she wouldn't be drinking.

That affirmed two things. One: Sasha felt it imperative that she remain stone-cold sober. Two: she didn't trust what she might do if she wasn't.

*All the better.*

That way there'd be no question of impropriety when they tumbled into his bed.

"Thank you for your vote of confidence." Jordan put a piece of the warm, flaky pastry oozing with cheese on each of their plates and handed her one. "But I know bloody well you didn't come to that conclusion from speaking to my parents."

Her gaze dropped to her plate for a moment. When it returned to his there was an unmistakable pity that made his cheeks burn.

"Your mother wouldn't have invested in my services if she didn't think your work worthy." Sasha skillfully avoided mention of Jonathan Jace's feelings about his art.

*Add kindness and compassion to the woman's growing list of virtues.*

"And as to my conclusions about you...well, I always make a point of arriving at those on my own. And what sealed it for me wasn't Jordan Jace, the artist. It was Jordan Jace, the man."

Jordan paused, a forkful of cheesy deliciousness inches from his lips, and cocked an eyebrow. "How do you mean?"

"I mean I'm impressed with your commitment to the environment and to helping disadvantaged young artists." She shrugged, breaking and spearing a piece of the pastry with her fork. "I've always been a sucker for a man with a cause." She nearly said the words under her breath.

Jordan chuckled. "Ahh...you were that girl. The one who wears her heart on her sleeve and has a 'Save The' sticker for every cause known to man."

"Am I that transparent?" Sasha laughed, then

took a bite of the pastry. Her murmur of appreciation went straight below his belt.

Jordan groaned internally, painfully aware of the need to adjust his trousers.

"I admit I'm a proud, card-carrying member of several organizations. Organizations and causes I care deeply about. The environment and funding arts education in public schools happen to be two of the causes I hold dear." She smiled. "So this isn't just a routine client job for me. It's important that I help you succeed."

There was something about the warmth of her words and the sincerity with which she uttered them that tugged at a string in his chest. The unexpected feeling temporarily rendered him speechless.

"All right, Sasha Charles. You win. I'd be a fool to turn down an offer like that." Jordan smiled. "So where exactly do we begin?"

"Two areas." Sasha opened the folder. "First, we make your social media accounts more dynamic and engaging. More reflective of you and your art."

"Sounds good." He nodded. "I'm sure Lydia will be glad to have that off her plate. Call my office during the week and she'll give you the log-in information for all of the accounts."

"My team will generate the posts, but I'll run everything past you. Get your approval first. Especially in the beginning while we're learning each other."

"Learning each other," he repeated her words, fondly. If that would require more evenings spent in the company of this gorgeous, compassionate woman, Jordan was all in. "I like the sound of that even better. Only I'm at quite the disadvantage. Aside from what you do for a living, I know very little about you."

"There's not much to tell." Sasha shrugged. "I'm an average girl from an average, working-class family. I grew up in a neighborhood where nothing was given, and everything was earned. I've been driven by that motto my entire life." She took another bite of the pastry. "End of story."

"That's a good start." Jordan couldn't help the admiration that rose in his chest as he surveyed the woman. "But somehow I feel you're being extremely modest. That there's a lot more than you're letting on."

"Can't give up all of my secrets right away." Sasha pulled another piece of the pastry off, creating a long, gooey string of cheese.

Jordan was enthralled with watching her place a morsel in her mouth and chew. He gulped water from his glass and set it on the table again. "So, what does an average girl from an average, working-class family like to do for fun?"

Her brown eyes danced with amusement. "When I'm not working or volunteering for a youth mentoring organization run by a friend, I'm usually hanging out with friends or visiting my family. Though, there haven't been many girls' nights out since my best friend, Miranda, married Vaughn Ellicott—a friend of yours, I believe."

Jordan's jaw tightened as he recalled his most recent encounter with Vaughn when he'd suspected him of being a vandal and thief.

"He's the treasurer of our local Prescott George chapter." There was no need to say more than that.

"You don't like him." Sasha tilted her head as she assessed him. It wasn't a question. "I wasn't sure I did either, at first. But when I realized he really, truly loved Miranda…well, then I gave him a fair chance. The better I know him, the more I like him."

"Perhaps I don't know him well enough yet." Jordan smiled politely, eager to move on from discussing Vaughn Ellicott. "My fault entirely, I'm sure. I'm not the most social member of the club."

"Being a member of Prescott George is quite an investment. And your membership there offers you the opportunity to make incredible connections locally and abroad. So as your brand strategist, I'd recommend that you become a more social member."

"Yes, ma'am," he grumbled as the server brought their meals and set them on the table. After they'd both had a chance to dig in to their meals, he returned his attention to her. "So, it's a Friday night.

You aren't working or volunteering and your best friend is spending time with her new husband. What would be your ideal way to spend the evening?"

"I'm a jeans and flip-flops kind of girl at heart." She looked up from her coq au vin for a moment. "So while I do like to dress up on occasion, I'm just as content to sit on my sofa and watch TV while drinking a light beer and eating takeout from a really good chicken shack. The kind you find in only the sketchiest of neighborhoods."

Jordan couldn't help the genuine laughter her statement evoked. "You're simply full of surprises, aren't you?"

"I could say the same of you." She smiled. "You're not just the rebellious wild child everyone thinks you are. You're a brilliant artist, well versed in your craft. You have a huge heart and a soft spot for kids who want to be artists, too. Kids who remind you of yourself."

When he didn't respond, she continued. "You pretend to be this perennial bad boy. And perhaps at some point you were. But that isn't the person I see."

Jordan shifted in his seat beneath her warm brown eyes. There was something about those eyes. They had the uncanny ability to peer beyond the surface. To bore a hole in the hardened exterior he was willing to show the world. To dig into the soft, vulnerable center he worked so hard to conceal.

It was unnerving.

He was accustomed to dealing with people at surface level. He kept them at a safe distance. Didn't dig too deep or allow them to.

Yet, here was Sasha Charles, barreling through all the barriers. Not fooled by the facade he showed to the world.

"And exactly who is it that you think you see?" He focused on cutting into his lamb chop.

"You're a really good guy, Jordan Jace. You care about the world and the people in your community. You're not the self-involved trust fund kid people think you are."

"Maybe that's exactly what I want them to see."

"But why? Why wouldn't you want people to see the truth? To realize what a good person you are?"

"I don't work with the kids for publicity. It's something I do for myself and for them. And philanthropist artists don't make for very splashy headlines. Think back to all the great artists. It's their stories of scandal and tragedy that you remember. Not that they helped little old ladies across the street." His voice had grown slightly tense.

He hadn't purposely created his bad boy image, but he hadn't done anything to discourage it, either. And he'd most certainly reveled in the freedom it afforded him. He was content to keep things just as they were.

"I guess you're right about the notoriety of some artists." Sasha nodded thoughtfully. "But I happen to believe that authenticity is more powerful. Why can't you embrace all of who you are? Playboy philanthropist could certainly be a thing. One that would work for you and make more corporations open their doors to your art for their public spaces."

Jordan sighed. "I'll think about it…on two conditions."

Sasha rolled her eyes, then put down her fork. The corner of her mouth curved in a smile she was doing a miserable job of hiding. "All right, let's hear it."

"No more business talk. We spend the rest of dinner 'learning each other.'"

"And the second condition?" She raised an eyebrow.

"Go out with me again tomorrow afternoon."

"Jordan…" She shook her head.

"You want to know more about me…as an artist and as a man? Then go out with me tomorrow. It won't be anything fancy. Dress just the way you would if you were spending the afternoon running errands or hanging with friends. But it will be worthwhile. I promise you."

Sasha sighed. She chewed her lower lip, her head tilted slightly as she assessed him. She pulled out her black planner, pen in hand, and scanned it.

"Fine. What time tomorrow afternoon?"

"I'll pick you up at two o'clock." Something inside his chest leaped for joy.

Sasha was definitely interested. The heat and passion in her eyes the night they met—that was no mere act. Nor was the effort she'd made to stay reserved. Calm. To act as if she were completely unaffected by him.

But there were little hints in her expression. In the tone of her voice.

She fancied him, too.

But then there was her penchant for propriety. Her hesitance to break her self-imposed rules. Enticing Sasha to venture beyond the safety of the barbed wire fence she'd erected around herself would require more than boyish charm or swagger.

Sasha wasn't impressed with his family name, his wealth or his fancy cars. Her excitement over his ability to secure the hottest restaurant reservations in town was mild at best.

What drew Sasha in was him opening up to her. Being genuine to the point of discomfort. Talking about subjects he normally avoided. Like disappointing his parents. Or the years he'd spent schlepping garbage and cleaning paintbrushes as an artist's apprentice. His work with underprivileged youth.

Sasha Charles was unlike any woman he'd known. Which made her more of a challenge and infinitely more desirable.

Everything in Jordan's life was a tad bit sweeter when he'd been forced to work for it. It was obvious Sasha Charles intended to make him do just that.

# Chapter 5

Sasha paced the floor of her apartment in a pair of khaki shorts, a cotton tank and her favorite pair of leather sandals.

*Going out with Jordan again is a mistake.*

Sasha recognized she was treading dangerous territory with Jordan Jace. She'd had countless client lunches and dinners. None of them left her feeling the way she had after spending two nights in Jordan's company.

She worked with clients that had left her angry, confused or both. But none of them were an enigmatic puzzle she was desperately compelled to solve. None of them made her want to keep tugging at strings until she'd found the one that would unravel him.

She checked the time on her phone.

*Too late to cancel now.*

Sasha sucked in a deep, belly breath. She released it, then repeated the entire process again and again.

Last night, she'd pretended, with great effort, to be completely nonchalant about Jordan's gorgeous, expensive car. And only mildly impressed by his ability to secure reservations to the hottest restaurant in town on short notice.

Truthfully, she'd been touched by the lengths to which Jordan had gone to impress her. And she was just as taken with him. In any other circumstance, she'd have happily encouraged his efforts. But this was business, and Jordan was a client.

*Still, he did look good enough to eat last night.*

Sasha sank her teeth into her lower lip, remembering how fine Jordan had looked and how delicious he'd smelled when he'd arrived at her door. Her skin had tingled and electricity trailed down her spine, igniting a warm sensation between her thighs. For the briefest moment, she'd wondered how it would feel to yank him inside her apartment and press her lips to his. Allow the hands of an artist to explore every part of her body.

Instead, she'd bitten the inside of her cheek,

pressed her lips into a hard line and greeted him as she would've greeted any other client.

Jordan's unmistakable knock on her door pulled her from her daze.

Even the man's knock was masculine and virulent and...*oh God*...there was that warmth and tingling in parts of her anatomy that insisted on going rogue.

"Hey." She opened the door, slightly stunned by what she saw. Jordan in a pair of slim cut, tattered jeans and a T-shirt that read King. His curly hair was worn in a full afro. Well-groomed, yet slightly unruly. Just enough to make her want to slide her fingers in it and pull his mouth to hers.

*Damn.*

There was that warmth and tingling again.

She needed to pull it together or it would be impossible to make it through the rest of their date that wasn't a date. At least, not in the traditional take-me-to-your-place-and-have-your-way-with-me sense. Though she couldn't help wishing it was.

"Hey." Jordan leaned against the doorway. His gaze trailed down her body and lingered on her legs for a moment before returning to meet hers. "You took my advice and kept it casual. Though, you've somehow managed to look just as stunning as you did last night in a cocktail dress."

Sasha's cheeks warmed and she mumbled her thanks as she quickly stepped into the hall. Before she could do something stupid. Like lean in and kiss him.

He surprised her by jumping into a discussion of her marketing plan the moment they got into the car. Jordan seemed to embrace the idea. Even if he didn't fully appreciate the need for the work she did, he seemed willing to give her plan a chance.

She'd been so distracted by their lively conversation about her ideas for honing his brand, that she hadn't noticed where they were. They weren't in the kind of affluent neighborhood a person like Jordan Jace normally frequented.

He'd been mysterious when she inquired about exactly where they were going. Now she understood why. He'd taken note of what she'd said the previous night about her ideal Friday night. It was Saturday afternoon, but she appreciated it just the same.

"We're going to a dive chicken shack." She couldn't help the smile that tightened her cheeks.

"It's actually a rib joint, but the chicken is quite good, too." Jordan looked straight ahead as he navigated the much narrower streets. "Hope that's all right."

"It's perfect." She resisted the urge to hug him.

The hole-in-the-wall restaurant had a line that went out the front door and around a corner. But it was worth every moment spent waiting in line.

Sasha was sure Jordan would want to take their food back to his place or to his studio. Instead, they shared a rickety picnic table with a family of four, including two adorable little girls.

They noshed on ribs, chicken, homemade potato salad, green beans and mouthwatering peach cobbler. Jordan was completely comfortable out of his usual element. He sparked conversation with their fellow diners, most of whom were from the surrounding neighborhood.

Sharing a meal like that, while enjoying a sense of community reminiscent of the small, working-class neighborhood she'd grown up in, she couldn't resist letting her guard down. They laughed, chatted and shared their food, as if they were old friends.

Sasha couldn't remember when she'd last felt so at ease with anyone outside of her circle of family and longtime friends.

*Too bad he's a client.*

Translation: look, but don't dare touch. No matter how badly she wanted to lean across the table and lick the dab of barbecue sauce that dotted the edge of his mouth. Her tongue glided across her lower lip, just thinking of it.

When she looked up, Jordan's gaze had zeroed in on her mouth and the movement of her tongue.

Sasha's face heated. She returned her attention to her food, sopping up a bit of the delicious sauce with a slice of white bread. Something she'd done since she was a child.

"Ice cream?" He gathered their empty food containers and put them in the trash.

"I couldn't eat another bite." Sasha patted her distended belly. "Not that ice cream doesn't sound good." She tossed their soda cans in the recycle bin and crossed the dusty, gravel lot beside him. "What I need is a good jog to burn off some of those calories."

"How about a brisk stroll instead?" He smiled, his eyes twinkling. There seemed to be some secret hidden behind his brown eyes.

Everything in her told her it was best if she said no, but she wasn't ready to end their afternoon together.

Maybe this wasn't a real date, but the three days she'd spent with Jordan were the best time she'd had…maybe ever.

"Lead the way."

Jordan set the alarm on his car and they strolled down a street with small, simple homes and compact, well-manicured yards.

"Thank you." Sasha walked beside him along a path that led to a brick school building.

"For lunch?"

"For being so thoughtful." Sasha's heart beat a little faster. She told herself it was because of the brisk walk. Not because of her proximity to Jordan Jace. "Last night you asked what I liked to do,

and today we did just that. Though this was probably the last thing in the world you wanted to do."

"You think this was my first time eating at that
little rib shack?" Jordan's words were filled with
amusement. "It happens to be one of my favorite
places to eat."

"How'd you come across it?"

"I don't just teach at my studio." He nodded toward the school they were approaching. "I've done
some special projects with students at this high
school, including that one."

"My God, Jordan. This is stunning." Sasha stared
at the mural that took up the lower half of one side
of the building. The vibrant colors popped, breathing life into a building that had seen better decades.
The mural consisted of six distinct panels.

"Each panel chronicles the story of a notable person who once attended this school before going on
to do something important." They walked along the
panels depicting a racially diverse group of people
including an artist, an engineer, two activists, an
inventor and a politician.

"Learning about each of them and the obsta-
cles they overcame was fascinating. Inspiring."
His brown eyes shone with pride. "But it was truly
an honor working with these students. Getting to
know them. They're so bright, and many of them
are dealing with issues at home you wouldn't believe." He shook his head sadly. "This project was

a respite from the storm for some of them. For others, it sparked something inside. Either because of the people they were learning about or because of the talent they discovered in themselves. It was a life-changing experience for me. I hope it was for them, too."

A pit of warmth welled in her chest as he spoke. She admired him even more. Her work with Jordan was about more than making him wealthier and more well-known. She could see that now. She'd do everything in her power to give him more opportunities to work on projects like this one.

"How'd you talk the school into diverting money to the project?"

"I didn't." Jordan shoved his hands in his pockets. "I made them an offer they couldn't refuse. I donated my services and the money for supplies."

Sasha's attention snapped to his. She'd read everything she could find on Jordan Jace. She hadn't read anything about his participation in this project or his donation.

"Why didn't you put out a press release or talk about the project on your website or any of your social media outlets?" She took out her phone. "I can only imagine how much this project must've meant to those students and to the neighborhood."

"That's just it... I did this for those kids and the neighborhood. Not to elevate myself to some sort of saint." He seemed perturbed by linking their objective to his.

Sasha snapped a few photos of the mural with her cell phone, then put it away and turned to Jordan.

"It's admirable you're not doing this for selfish reasons. And I applaud your willingness to give your time, money and expertise without expecting anything in return." Sasha smiled warmly. "But think of it as a symbiotic relationship. Neither entity is using the other. You're working together to do more good in the world than either of you could alone."

Jordan turned toward the mural again. He studied it in silence for a moment. "I don't see how publicizing it will be helpful. This is a painting. I'm a sculptor."

"Doesn't matter." Sasha was relieved Jordan was seriously considering her suggestion. "I can still make it work, benefitting both you and the school."

"How?"

"You get positive press and perhaps we can get other artists and corporations to participate in or fund similar projects at this school and others. We can expand what you started here beyond the scope of the limited number of students you can personally help. You'd like that, wouldn't you?"

"Of course."

"Then trust me." Sasha placed a hand on his arm and he turned to her. His heated gaze held hers and the space between them seemed to contract. She swallowed hard. "I promise not to compromise the kids or the community."

"I do trust you." Jordan extended his hand. He shook hers when she placed it in his palm. "And I look forward to working with you."

Jordan didn't release her hand. His gaze still locked with hers, his mouth inched closer to hers.

Sasha froze. Her breath came harder and faster, and her head felt light. She couldn't look away from his mesmerizing gaze. Or step outside of the space between them, growing ever smaller.

*This is inappropriate on every level.*

Jordan Jace was a client. A fine one with ultra-kissable lips. Eyes that drew you in. A gravelly voice that made her most intimate parts hypersensitive.

She wanted Jordan to kiss her. Needed an answer to the question that'd circulated in her brain and lit a fire in her flesh from the moment he'd trained his eyes on her that night at the gallery.

*What would it feel like to kiss him?*

"Jordan, I ca—" She stepped backward and tripped over the uneven sidewalk.

"Got you." He grabbed her before she hit the ground and cradled her in his strong arms. Sasha inhaled his scent—smooth and spicy with a hint of vanilla. "You didn't hurt yourself, did you?"

*Just wounded what little of my pride there was left.*

"I'm fine." Sasha righted herself. Her heart raced as much from her proximity to Jordan as the near fall. "Thank you. I swear, I'm not usually such a klutz."

His dark eyes danced in the sunlight. "So either I make you nervous in a good way or you desperately want to be rid of me. I'm hoping it's the former not the latter."

"If you must know, it's both." She extracted herself from his arms.

"So, because I make you nervous, in a good way, you're desperate to be rid of me." Deep in thought, he scratched the stubble on his chin, which only made him more enticing. "Can't decide if that's the best bloody compliment anyone has ever given me or if I should be mortified by the insult."

"It's neither a compliment nor an insult. It's a statement of fact." She took one more glance at the incredible mural before turning back to him. "It's getting late. We should head back to the car."

"If that's what you want." For the first time, he seemed slightly unsure of himself. "Look, I hope I didn't offend you just now by trying to kiss you."

"You didn't." Sasha folded her arms. Her gaze swept the ground until she drew up enough courage to meet his eyes again. "I don't deny that I'm flattered by your interest. And I like you. A lot. Under any other circumstances…" She sighed heavily. "But this isn't any other circumstance. You're my client. An important one. I can't afford to…to…" *Blow it. Screw up… Why can't I think of a term without a sexual connotation?* "Ruin… I can't afford to ruin this opportunity."

"Is there a rule that precludes you from dating a client?"

"Not technically, but it would seem improper."

"To whom?"

"To me and, I'm sure, to your mother who, let's not forget, is paying my rather hefty consultation fee."

"Did my mum tell you that?"

"The impropriety of dating her son didn't come up in our initial discussion, no," she said flippantly.

"Pity." Jordan grinned. "I would've loved to hear her opinion on the matter. Not that it would've swayed mine. And from where I stand, the only opinions that matter on the subject are yours and mine."

"This isn't just about how it would look to everyone at my firm and to other potential clients. Getting involved with you romantically would be a disastrous idea."

"Ouch." Jordan pressed a hand to his chest, in mock pain. "You haven't the slightest regard for my overinflated ego."

"I didn't mean it that way." She readjusted the

purse slung across her body. "But it would ruin our working relationship."

"I disagree." A mischievous smirk made him even more handsome. "Last night you said we needed to learn each other. I can't think of a better way to accomplish that."

"You're awful." She couldn't help laughing, though the last thing she should be doing is encouraging him. Sasha turned back up the path toward the car. "I admit it, I enjoy hanging out with you, Jordan. But I think it's best that we keep these meetings strictly about business."

"Isn't that what we were just doing?" He jerked a thumb over his shoulder toward the mural.

"Right up until you tried to kiss me, and I nearly let you."

Sasha had wanted a taste of those sensual, full lips from the first time he'd flashed her his impish grin. But her career and the reputation she'd built were more important than her sensual curiosity about a man like Jordan Jace. A man whose lovers were as disposable as single-use contact lenses.

"Fair enough." He nodded. "What's our next matter of business?"

"We need to finalize your brand strategy. Could we get together on Monday or Tuesday for our initial meeting, then again later in the week to finalize the plan?"

"Not possible."

"I promised your mother I'd give your account priority." She produced her ever-present planner. "So I'm willing to be flexible on when and where we meet to accommodate any possible scheduling conflicts."

Impressing the Jace family matriarch could bring her a slew of well-heeled clients on both sides of the Atlantic Ocean. If that meant making a few concessions to her reluctant new client, it was worth the trade-off.

"I'm not trying to be difficult, I assure you. I just happen to already have..." Jordan paused mid-sentence, his eyes suddenly gleaming and a grin spreading across his face. "I was going to say we can't meet because I'll be traveling next week. But I just had a brilliant idea. You should come with me. I'm going to Mazatlán by boat. It's a working holiday. Not nearly as glamorous as it might sound."

"Too bad. Glamorous sounds fun."

Being stuck on a dirty, old fishing boat for the next several days wasn't her idea of a good time. And the fluttering in her belly at the possibility of spending time alone with Jordan Jace was a flashing red sign. Still, this was the perfect opportunity to demonstrate to Eva Jace her willingness to go above and beyond to accommodate the needs of her clients.

There was just one thing she needed to clarify. "Why do you want me to come along?"

"I've an idea for a new series of smaller sculptures. Something that would be more accessible to discriminating private art buyers. It occurred to me that it would be beneficial for you to be privy to my entire process—from start to finish."

Jordan's cunning smile and the gleam in his eye betrayed his strictly business logic about the trip. Still, he had a point. It would help her get to know him better as an artist, allowing her to tailor a plan that would fit Jordan's unique sensibilities.

"When would we leave?"

His smile widened. "Bright and early on Tuesday morning."

*Of course.* She'd have little more than two days to prepare.

"I'll have my assistant contact yours to make arrangements." She jotted down notes in her planner, then tapped out a message on her phone.

"While she's at it…there are a few other dates we should go ahead and plan, too." Jordan grinned broadly. His use of the word *date* was no Freudian slip of the tongue. He enjoyed teasing her.

And, if she was being honest, she was eager to spend more time with the surprising Jordan Jace.

## Chapter 6

"What do you think?" Jordan gestured toward the incredible, three-story, luxury yacht they'd be sharing for the next week.

Sasha's eyes widened as she surveyed the large, gleaming vessel and its crew standing on deck, ready to serve their every need. Her mouth fell open.

She was clearly impressed, whether she was willing to admit it or not.

"*This* is the 'little boat'?"

"You object?"

"It's incredible. But all of this…" she stammered, indicating the ten-person, luxury yacht. "It's just for us?"

"Us and the diligent eight-person crew that comes with it." He stepped aside, nodding his thanks to two crew members who began loading their luggage onto the ship.

Her eyes widened and her cheeks flushed. "I can't... I mean, I shouldn't—"

"Relax, love. If you're worried that I'm squandering my fortune in an effort to woo you...don't. The ship belongs to a friend." Jordan pulled his shades from his breast pocket and put them on. "And if you've any qualms about our sleeping arrangements..." He swallowed a grin as she gasped quietly and the flush of her cheeks deepened. "There are four staterooms, in addition to the master suite, so you needn't worry."

"All right, then. I'm in." Sasha released a long, slow breath and nodded, still surveying the regal vessel. "But regardless of how glamorous this yacht may be, this is a working trip for me, not a vacation."

"Well, we must see what we can do to remedy that." Jordan tried his best to restrain a grin. "I know you're quite dedicated, but I'm sure we can manage to fit a bit of fun into the next seven days."

Her expression softened slightly and a smile curved one edge of her mouth. "I suppose you're right. After all, who knows when I'll get another opportunity like this. But work comes first. No exceptions."

"Agreed." He extended his elbow, escorted her up the gangway stairs and to her lovely stateroom.

Jordan made his way to the master suite and settled in, a smile plastered on his face. By the end of their trip down to Mazatlán and Puerto Vallarta, he had every intention of helping Sasha Charles learn to loosen up a bit. Preferably in his bed.

Sasha tucked the last of her clothing into a built-in dresser in her generously appointed stateroom. As beautiful and spacious as the room was, she couldn't imagine how decadent the master suite must be.

Nor did she have any intention of finding out.

Jordan occupied the master suite near the bow of the yacht, while her room was located near the stern. Beneath them, a small village of crew members were busy preparing their lunch, which would be served on deck shortly.

Sasha paced the cabin filled with warm sunlight. Fresh sea air filtered in through the door of the small, private balcony.

She was on an incredible ship, taking an all-expenses-paid cruise to Mazatlán and Puerto Vallarta. A heavenly scent wafted through the space, courtesy of two large bouquets of red roses and pink Asiatic lilies and gerbera daisies.

Sasha inhaled the calming scent. Breathed in and out as her pulse slowed down.

It was clear why Jordan's mother had hired her.

The bad boy, demanding artist image the public had of him was completely wrong.

Jordan was incredibly smart, intensely passionate about his art and exceedingly committed to the causes he cared about. Her opinion of him had improved greatly upon getting to know him.

She admired him. Wanted him.

Admiring a client was ideal. Desiring him and wondering how it would've felt if she'd let him kiss her probably weren't the best uses of her time.

*Keep it professional and everything will be fine.*

After all, Jordan Jace wasn't the first wealthy, handsome client she'd worked with. He wasn't even the first to flirt with her.

So why did everything about working with Jordan feel different?

Sasha's knee bounced involuntarily and her belly twisted in knots. She tried to push Jordan from her mind. But when she closed her eyes, all she could see was his handsome face.

Narrow, deep-set eyes. A wide, generous smile that usually hinted at the mischief that always seemed to be happening inside that beautiful man's head. Intense eyes and a heart-stopping smile.

Today he'd worn his hair in soft twists in the crown, while the sides were cut low. He looked like he'd stepped out of a nautical clothing catalog in a navy shirt with white polka dots, white shorts and navy boat shoes.

The light, fitted attire highlighted his strong biceps, muscular thighs and incredibly toned bottom. Heat made its way down her spine and pooled low in her belly as she imagined how enticing his body must look beneath his clothing. Radiant brown skin, rippling with muscles underneath. A smattering of fine hair.

Her neck and chest flushed with arousal, and her nipples beaded painfully.

Sasha paced the floor, her heart thudding. She'd committed to spending seven days sailing the seas virtually alone with Jordan Jace.

*What an arrogant, boneheaded mistake.*

She'd gone on lots of working trips with other clients—both male and female. And she was determined to prove that Jordan Jace was no different.

But it was a lie she'd been trying to sell herself on, when all along she knew the truth. This trip was very different because Jordan was unlike any man she'd ever known.

She'd gone on past client trips begrudgingly, despite the exotic locations. But when Jordan had proposed this trip, her heart leaped in her chest. She relished the opportunity to have Jordan all to herself for an entire week.

Eyes pressed closed, she released a deep sigh. She'd screwed up royally.

"Sasha." Jordan knocked at the door. "Are you ready?"

She took another deep breath before opening the door and greeting him with a big smile. As if everything was fine. "Yes."

His gaze dropped momentarily to the pebbled nubs visible through the gauzy, yellow material of her sundress. Jordan cleared his throat and rubbed the back of his neck.

"Thought you might need an escort to the sundeck where we're having lunch." He looked anywhere but her eyes or at her chest. Crimson bloomed beneath the brown skin on his cheeks. "Just until you learn your way around the ship."

Sasha thanked Jordan and joined him in the hall. He led her to the sundeck where a lovely alfresco meal of seafood pasta was served.

He helped her into her chair, then took a seat across from her.

Their pasta was divine, and she enjoyed Jordan's company, as always. When they'd finished their meal, the chief stewardess cleared their places, leaving a small platter of fruit and two small plates.

Sasha scanned the full lips that had been such a distraction all afternoon. Regret bubbled in her chest. For a moment, she couldn't quite remember why she hadn't let Jordan Jace kiss her.

Jordan shifted under Sasha's heated gaze. He clenched, then unclenched his fists. Reminded himself to stay the course.

The cruise was only the beginning. He had big plans for Sasha Charles as they sailed to Mexico and back. But his plans would implode if he rushed her.

He wanted to kiss her. To pull her onto his lap in that yellow sundress and claim the soft lips that had taunted him for the past hour. Tease the pert nipples that had been peeking through the thin material, tantalizing him. Making his mouth water with his spiraling need for her.

*Patience, mate. Don't be so direct, so predictable.*

Sasha seemed to anticipate him trying to kiss her again. And from the way she'd been staring longingly at his mouth throughout their meal, he'd no doubt that another attempt to kiss her would receive a much different response.

He wasn't sure why Sasha's rebuff that day haunted him so. He had a king-size ego, to be sure. But he wasn't so arrogant as to believe he was the pot of gold at the end of every woman's rainbow.

Something about Sasha Charles had burrowed its way beneath his skin and gotten cozy. He'd found himself focused on her at the most importune times. Like when another woman was openly flirting with him. Yet, all he'd been able to think of was Sasha.

Her remarkable smile. Her biting sense of humor. The lightness that rose in his chest whenever he was in her company.

Jordan released a quiet sigh. Part frustration with

himself for his preoccupation with Sasha. Part admiration for the woman who engendered such adoration.

A saner man would cut his losses, put his wounded pride in his pocket and walk away. But his curiosity had the better of him. He needed to understand exactly what it was about Sasha Charles that made him so crazy. And he was willing to bet there was something about him that made Sasha crazy, too.

So, to avoid another polite rejection, he wouldn't attempt to kiss her. Not because his ego was too fragile to sustain such an objection. Because he relished the idea of making her want him enough that she would relinquish her self-imposed rules.

"Ready to review the branding strategy?" It hurt him to suggest something so sensible. Especially when he couldn't get the image of her nipples straining against her sundress out of his head.

"You actually want to work on the plan?" She looked bewildered. Perhaps even disappointed. "Right now?"

"It's as good a time as any." Jordan sipped his ginger beer. He'd taken a play from Sasha's playbook. He was determined to keep his head clear. He would follow the plan, rather than giving in to his impulses where she was concerned.

She opened her phone and reviewed some of her ideas for making over his website, social media accounts and gallery marketing materials. They made him inexplicably uneasy. Not because they weren't brilliant ideas. Because they were brilliant ideas for someone else.

"I don't fancy the idea of allowing the general public into my life, into my process." Jordan shifted in his chair. "Take away the heavy curtain, and where's the magic? It's gone, because there's no mystery left to solve."

"I appreciate your thinking on this. I really do. But ravenous fans—the kind you want—they want access. They want to know what you do and how your mind works. They want to know where you eat, what kind of clothes you wear and where your inspiration comes from."

"I don't think I'd want to know all of that about anyone. It'd bore me to tears. Don't these people have lives of their own?"

"Most do. For them, living vicariously through someone else is an escape. A fun way to spend a few minutes here or there. For others, it's a way to feel a sense of kinship with an artist they admire. It deepens their connection, making them a loyal fan who'll buy from you again and again."

"I'm sure you're right, but I prefer the days when one needn't post photos of one's breakfast in order to sell a sculpture." He leaned back in his seat. "What does it matter what I eat for breakfast or with whom I take it? And why should it matter what designer I'm wearing or where I vacation?"

"Consumers want openness and authenticity. They want to know who the real Jordan Jace is… beyond the bad boy image you project to everyone. What motivates you? Is it the money and the fame? Or is it the opportunity to give your parents the middle finger by achieving success without them while doing something they don't respect?"

"Are you asking because it's pertinent to my brand, or are you asking for yourself?" He shifted in his seat, unnerved by her spot-on analysis.

"Both, I guess." She shrugged. "After all, one feeds the other."

"All of the above." Jordan's throat tightened and his lungs constricted. Why was he so bothered by Sasha Charles thinking ill of him? "But you've neglected the most important motivator. My passion for the art itself. Whatever else you might think of me, Sasha, you must realize how very committed I am to what I do. That every single sculpture I create, commissioned or not, bears a small piece of me."

"That's exactly what I'm talking about." Sasha's eyes lit up as her fingers moved quickly across her mobile screen. "That's the kind of passion and transparency we need to bring to your brand."

"Look, Sasha, I appreciate what you're trying to do. I honestly do. I can see why my mother was so taken with you. You're quite brilliant." Jordan walked over to the railing and leaned against it, his arms folded. "But I've no intention of fundamentally changing who I am. For anyone or any reason."

"You think my job is to change you? It isn't. And that's not what I'm asking at all." Sasha grabbed a slice of mango and joined him at the railing. She bit into the sweet, fragrant fruit and chewed thoughtfully. "The problem isn't who you are and what you represent. It's that people don't really know who you are or what you represent." Sasha's voice softened and she gave him a look of pity. "That includes your parents."

Jordan's jaw tensed and he sighed. "I don't much care what my parents think, and I've given up trying to appease them. They won't be satisfied with anything short of me dying a thousand deaths of boredom while lost in spreadsheets all day like my brothers. It's fine for them, but it isn't me. And it never will be. Not ever. So, if the point of all this is to slowly transform me into a boring old f—"

Sasha reached out and pressed her hand to his mouth, her fingers sweet and sticky with the mango juice. Her sudden action seemed to take them both by surprise.

She withdrew her hand, her chest quickly rising and falling. "I'm sorry. I shouldn't have done that. I don't know what I was thinking. I mean, obviously, I wasn't really thinking at all. I just needed you to stop talking for one minute and actually listen to what it is I'm trying to say to you."

"And exactly what is it you are trying to say?"

"That I don't want you to change. Because I think you're remarkable. You're smart and you're handsome and God are you talented." The admiration and affection in her eyes made his chest swell. "You're an amazing artist, Jordan, and an even better man. So no, I'm not asking you to change. I'm saying we need to better communicate who you are and what you're about."

It was the loveliest, most sincere thing anyone had ever said to him. Stated by the most pleasing, yet perplexing woman he'd ever met.

"Kind of you to say." He finally broke their silence. "And I don't mean to be difficult."

"No, of course not. Ultimately, it's your image and reputation and you want to protect it. I can certainly respect that."

"Good." Jordan nodded once. "In which case, I promise to trust you and follow your lead on this."

He licked his lower lip, tasting the mango juice she'd left there. His focus shifted to her mouth, and his desire to taste her lips. He stuffed his hands into his pockets.

Space, he needed space.

"Seems we're done here. If you need anything, anything at all, ring the chief stewardess. She'll get you whatever it is you need."

"You're leaving?" She frowned.

"It's a working holiday, after all. I'll be sketching most of the evening and late into the night."

"So I'm on my own for dinner?" Her voice was tinged with disappointment.

"Wouldn't be so rude as to make you eat alone your first night onboard." He smiled. "But I'm taking dinner in my suite while I work. You're welcome to join me there, if you'd like. I'll try to take a break round eight."

Sasha narrowed her gaze, her lips pursed. She nodded. "See you at eight."

"Perfect." He leaned in a little closer. "I have one rule about dinner tonight. We don't talk business."

"Isn't that the point of me being here?"

"During the day, I'm your client and you're my branding strategist. During the evening, we're two people on their own time, getting to know one another. Deal?"

Sasha chewed her lower lip, her nose scrunched. Then she nodded. "Deal. And I really am sorry about putting my hand over your mouth earlier. That isn't like me. I'm not sure what came over me, but it won't happen again."

"In the event that it does, I prefer pineapple." He winked, then walked away.

Sasha smoothed her skirt down, closed her eyes and took a deep breath.

*Eyes above his neck, hands to yourself and everything will be fine.*

She lifted her hand, pausing a moment before knocking on the door. No answer. She waited a bit, then knocked again. Harder this time. Still no answer.

Jordan had made it clear they wouldn't be discussing business. So, if he'd bailed on their dinner date, she could eat in her own stateroom, answer a few emails and maybe do some client work. Or she could binge watch one of the many television series she needed to catch up on.

Neither was a bad option when set on a ship as gorgeous as this one.

So why was she crushed by the possibility that Jordan had decided he had something better to do tonight?

The door swung open suddenly, taking her by surprise.

"Sorry, love. I hopped in the shower and time got away from me." Jordan tugged a black T-shirt down over his strong, taut abs. "Hope you weren't waiting long."

*Eyes above the neck. Eyes above the neck.*

"Not at all." Sasha quickly raised her eyes to his. "But if this is a bad time…"

"Your timing is perfect." Jordan looked beyond her at the staff rolling a cart toward them. He held the door open wider, stepping aside to let them enter.

"Jordan, this suite is amazing." Sasha's gaze swept around the bright, open, two-story master suite.

A spiral staircase anchored the center of the room. A shiny, black baby grand piano dominated one corner. And the stateroom had its own private sundeck.

"I can see why you enjoy working here." She gestured toward the easel set up near the observation deck. "I'd be inspired working here, too."

"I don't normally use this particular vessel for my working holidays, but I like to take them a couple of times each year. Gives me time alone, a chance to think and a fresh perspective."

"Then I'm intruding on your creative holiday, aren't I?"

"I invited you here." He braced her shoulders. His voice was low and sincere. His dark eyes shone. "I wouldn't have, if I didn't want your company."

A sense of relief crept down Sasha's spine, even as her body tensed from being so close to Jordan. His warmth and captivating scent drew her closer like an insect in summer drawn to the front porch light.

"Thank you for having me." Her words were barely louder than a whisper.

"Will that be all for now, Mr. Jace?" The chief stewardess seemed reluctant to interrupt them.

Jordan excused himself to speak with the woman privately, and Sasha went to the sundeck. The view was lovely, and the water was calming. A cool, salty breeze rustled her skirt. The sheer, white curtains billowed around her.

She smoothed down her skirt and turned around to meet Jordan's gaze. He leaned against the wall, his arms folded as he watched her. Her cheeks warmed and her stomach flipped as she held his heated gaze, neither of them speaking.

"Dinner's ready." He pulled out a chair at the small table near the sundeck. "I decided to forego full service tonight. I thought it would give us a chance to talk. Hope you don't mind."

"No, of course not." She took her seat as he uncovered their meals. Fresh lobster, crab and scallops, and a creamy, mushroom risotto. "Everything looks incredible, Jordan. Thank you for accommodating me for dinner tonight. It looks like you were busy. I'm sorry if our meal is interrupting your creative burst."

Jordan sat across from her, spread his napkin and put it in his lap. "Don't be. You're the reason I've been feeling so inspired lately."

"Me?" Butterflies flitted in her belly. "Why?"

"That's one of the reasons I invited you along on this trip." He poured them both a glass of wine. "I hope to unravel the mystery. One way or another."

Sasha's cheeks flamed, and she gulped down some of the water she was drinking, to extinguish the heat rising in her core.

"Tell me more about this series of sculptures you're working on." Better to avoid delving into the meaning of his statement.

Jordan gave her a knowing smile and sipped a little of his wine. "Remember my one rule for dinner? We don't discuss business."

"Right." She took a bite of her gourmet meal and murmured with delight.

Jordan's eyes darkened in response and he drank a little more of his wine before setting the glass down. He picked up his utensils and took the first bite.

"You told me about your family and that you grew up here in San Diego. How'd you become best friends with Vaughn's wife, Miranda? She's from Chicago, isn't she?"

"We went to college together and hit it off as freshmen. Been friends ever since, though we hadn't seen each other in a while before Miranda moved here."

"How long ago was that?"

"Shortly before she met Vaughn."

Sasha needn't go into details about how Miranda had come to San Diego in search of a husband. Or how her marriage of convenience to Vaughn turned into a real, genuine love.

The kind she wanted for herself someday.

Sasha had done her stint with casual dating. She was over it. Watching Vaughn and Miranda together was a revelation. She wanted a love like theirs. Or at least a serious relationship that could potentially lead to love and marriage.

She was done wasting her time with men who still acted like college frat boys. Determined to sleep their way across campus.

Men like Jordan Jace, if the rumors on blogs and online magazines were any indication.

Then again, upon deeper inspection, she'd found her initial perception of Jordan to be all wrong.

Maybe she was wrong about this, too.

"Speaking of friends…you seem to have quite a lot. Women friends, that is." She speared a succulent scallop. "It's amazing you find time to sculpt."

His gaze narrowed and his lips pressed together in a smirk as he watched her eat. He took a sip of his water and set the glass down.

"If there's something you need to ask me, Sasha, please do. I've nothing to hide." He took a bite of his meal.

Her mouth suddenly felt dry and a knot tightened in her stomach. "I thought we weren't discussing business tonight."

"And how is an inquiry into my love life related to our business dealings?" He tilted his head, assessing her.

"Everything. Because your mother didn't just hire me to help build your business. She and your father were adamant that I focus on cleaning up your reputation."

His eyes widened and he put his utensils down with a clang.

Sasha put her fork down, too. She raised a hand. "Before you get angry with me or them, let me explain."

Jordan folded his arms. "I'm listening."

"Your mother truly does believe that you're a talented artist. That you could easily become a global superstar. A household name."

"I find that difficult to believe." Jordan's brows knitted, his tone caustic.

"It's true." Sasha smiled softly, remembering her conversation with Eva Jace. "I know a proud mother when I see one."

"And do proud mums usually send someone out to 'fix' their children's reputations?" His nostrils flared.

"Sometimes." She shrugged, then sighed. "Look, your mother simply believes that your reputation of being demanding and…well, difficult, might be hampering you from being offered some incredible opportunities. And…"

"And…what?" Jordan folded his arms on the table as he leaned forward, head tilted.

"And she'd like to see you get some positive press for a change. Rather than stories about you and your flavor of the month." Sasha's cheeks stung with heat.

"My mother wants me to settle down and give her grandchildren." He took another bite of his food. "Not interested."

His adamant response felt like a punch to the gut.

"Monogamy isn't your thing, I assume." She tried not to sound like a kid who'd just learned that Santa and the Easter Bunny weren't real.

He grunted. "Bucks human nature, as evidenced by the astronomical divorce rate."

"Your parents seem happy together, as do mine. And Vaughn and Miranda—"

"Barely know each other." He sighed, sitting back in his chair. "I know she's your best friend. So I'm sorry to say it, but it's true."

"They make each other happy." She shoved her food around her plate, her appetite suddenly gone.

"For now." He put a forkful of food in his mouth. "Don't get me wrong, Sasha. I don't wish ill of them at all. Quite the contrary. I'd love it if they were to prove me wrong. And I wish them eternal happiness together."

"But you don't really believe it's possible. And it isn't something you'd want for yourself." Sasha stabbed a poor, defenseless shrimp. Her fork clanged against the dish, drawing Jordan's attention.

Heat swept up the back of her neck and across

her cheeks as he assessed her with something akin to pity.

"Look, I didn't mean to upset you. But you asked me a question and I answered it truthfully." His voice was softer. Apologetic. "I'd think that's what you'd want. For me to be honest."

"It is, of course." She forced a cursory smile. "I just think it's… I don't know…sad. That's all."

Jordon put down his fork and cocked his head. "You think I'm the pitiful one because I don't believe in some fairy-tale eternal love that has failed half the general population?" He sounded amused. "That's rich. I've always considered it to be the other way around."

"You feel sorry for Vaughn and Miranda?"

"Not them specifically, but folks in general who spend most of their lives unhappy, in search of something as rare as sightings of Sasquatch."

"Do you really believe that? That love is an unobtainable impossibility?" She wanted to be indignant, but instead her heart broke for him.

He sighed heavily. "Life is far too short to waste it on something that may or may not happen for me. I'd rather live each day to its fullest. Take life as it comes. I'm less apt to be disappointed that way."

"Hmm…" Sasha nodded. Suddenly things seemed quite clear.

"That was a sound full of meaning, if ever I heard one." He forced a smile. "Let me guess, you've come up with some brilliant analysis of exactly what my problem is."

"You could say that."

"And will you leave me twisting in the wind, or do you care to share with the class?" His eyes twinkled with amusement.

"I think you're scared. Terrified, in fact. Godzilla's coming, run-for-your-life scared."

"Scared? Of what? Do tell."

"Of getting your heart broken." She shrugged. "Same as the rest of us. Only, the rest of us are brave enough to take the chance."

Jordan was no longer amused. He narrowed his gaze and gulped some of his water.

"You think I'm frightened of having my feelings hurt? Failure and disappointment...that's part of life, love. I often take risks with my work. One can't be avant-garde without the nads to buck a few trends."

"True. But it takes more courage to be vulnerable to someone and truly let them into your life, doesn't it?"

"We're as different as chalk and cheese in some regards, yet..." Jordan tapped one finger on the table as he assessed her. He seemed to be carefully debating his next words. "Look, Sasha, I might as well put my cards on the table. You know how very attracted I am to you. Am I wrong in thinking you feel the same?"

Sasha swallowed hard. Her heart raced and her pulse pounded in her ears. "You're a client, and I don't get involved with my clients. Regardless of how I feel about them personally."

"And how do you feel about me...personally?" The amusement had returned to his voice and to those captivating eyes.

"It doesn't matter."

"It does to me," he insisted.

She sighed. "Fine. Yes, I'm attracted to you. I find you handsome and intriguing. I'm floored by your talent and moved by your concern for the environment and your willingness to mentor young artists."

"So why not explore our mutual admiration and have a bit of fun together?" His hand crept closer to hers on the table. "Because I'm quite taken with you, Sasha. I think we would get on well together."

"I'm not interested in a casual fling," she said abruptly, debating whether to put all her cards on the table, too. "I've been there and done that too many times before. I want something real. I want what Vaughn and Miranda have. And I could never have that with you because you've made it quite clear that isn't what you want."

"I see." He lowered his gaze briefly before it returned to hers. "And you're quite sure you wouldn't consider it?"

"I'm sorry if that means this trip is a waste for you."

"Not at all." The disappointment in his eyes belied his warm smile. "You're a fascinating woman, Sasha. And I quite enjoy your company, regardless of the circumstances."

Sasha smiled, relieved. They enjoyed the rest of their meal in cordial, relaxed conversation. Still, she couldn't let go of the small hope that Jordan might change his mind.

"One more thing," Jordan said. "I'd like you to be my guest at a private event I'm hosting at Sorella next week."

"What kind of event?"

"It's a mixer for Prescott George. I offered to host it after we talked about my being more social in the group."

She grinned. Maybe Jordan Jace wasn't a lost cause, after all. "I'd love to."

## Chapter 7

Sasha handed the valet her keys and followed the red carpet to the front door of Jordan's gallery, Sorella.

She traced the elegant gold flourish along the edge of the heavy, black linen imprinted with a fancy, gold font. Her invitation to the Prescott George event Jordan was hosting.

Sasha handed her invitation to the hostess working the front door and stepped inside. Soft jazz played over the speakers, and the space was already filling up with well-dressed, affluent people. Many of whom she recognized from their glossy magazine covers and feature articles in business journals.

"Ms. Charles, you made it." Lydia's obligatory smile more closely resembled a frown, and her voice was tight. She shoved her glasses up the bridge of her nose. "Jordan asked me to apologize for not greeting you himself. He's meeting with a few fellow Prescott George members. He'll find you when he has a free moment."

"Thank you, Lydia." Sasha scanned the room. "Have my friends Vaughn and Miranda Ellicott arrived yet?"

"Yes. In fact, Vaughn is one of the people he's meeting with in his office. His wife went upstairs a few minutes ago."

"Thank you, Lydia."

Initially, she'd been miffed at Lydia's chilly treatment. But looking in the woman's eyes now, she clearly understood.

Lydia was in love with Jordan and considered her a threat. Sasha could hardly blame her.

It took everything she had to maintain her distance during their time together at sea. She'd succeeded in keeping her hands off Jordan, but he'd been on her mind constantly. And she'd enjoyed every moment they spent together during their seven-day excursion.

By the end of the trip, he hadn't persuaded her of the benefits of a harmless fling and she hadn't convinced him of the benefits of a long-term relationship.

They'd ended the trip in the same place they began. Frustrated and desperately wanting each other. Only, her feelings for him had grown deeper. Because they'd spent their free time hanging together. Watching movies. Swimming in the ocean. Sightseeing in Mazatlán and Puerto Vallarta.

Each moment had made her feel closer to Jordan and want him even more.

She felt sorry for the woman. Almost as sorry as she felt for herself.

"My relationship with Jordan is strictly professional, you know."

"I'm sure you believe that, Ms. Charles." Lydia shoved her glasses up again. "But Jordan certainly doesn't."

The woman walked away, her pumps clicking angrily against the hardwood floors before Sasha could say anything more.

Sasha made her way through the growing crowd of people and up to the second floor.

"Miranda." She approached her friend studying one of Jordan's large sculptures.

"Sasha!" Miranda wrapped her in a tight hug, then squeezed her hand. "I didn't realize you'd be here tonight."

"I was invited by a client," Sasha said cryptically.

"So you're the one working with Jordan Jace. Why didn't you tell me that before?"

"You know I don't talk about my clients, unless they've given me the okay." Sasha smoothed down her skirt.

"Well, then, let's not talk about Jordan the client. Let's talk about Jordan Jace the very sexy brotha." Miranda snickered, dodging Sasha when she tried to shush her.

"His assistant already hates me," Sasha whispered loudly. "I reassured her that my relationship with Jordan is strictly business."

"I'm not buying it." Miranda studied Sasha's expression as she sipped her glass of wine. "The moment I mentioned him your cheeks got bright red and you're acting all nervous."

Sasha folded her arms and blew a stream of air through her pursed lips. She shrugged. "Yes, he's handsome and sexy and brilliant and funny. But he's also a notorious player who doesn't do relationships. Sure, he's interested in hooking up, but what then? I'm over the whole casual dating scene. I want what you and Vaughn have."

"Oh, honey." Miranda's expression went from playful to serious. "I didn't realize... I never would've teased you if I'd known—"

"If you'd known what?"

"That you're really, really into him." Miranda lowered her voice as she looked around.

"Is it that obvious?" Heat crawled up Sasha's neck and face. She didn't bother denying it. Her friend could see right through the lies she'd been trying to tell herself. "No wonder his assistant wasn't convinced."

Miranda beamed. "No, I just know you that well. And I can't remember the last time I heard you speak so glowingly of any man. Jordan made quite an impression on you."

Sasha sighed. "It doesn't matter. He's a client. Even if he weren't, I'm not interested in another meaningless fling."

"Those can be fun, too." Miranda wiggled her eyebrows, and they both laughed. "But if you really like him, don't give up so quickly. Maybe Jordan doesn't believe in getting serious because he hasn't encountered the right woman yet."

"I've made that mistake before." Sasha guided her friend away from two couples that had come to look at the sculpture. "It never ends well, and I don't want to waste my time anymore."

"Miss Charles, there you are."

Sasha turned toward the familiar voice. She smiled at the older woman dressed in a black Chanel suit pinned with a diamond brooch that likely cost more than Sasha made in a year.

*Eva Jace.* Jordan's mother. Accompanied by his father, Jonathan Jace.

Sasha introduced them to Miranda, who took her leave and returned to the main floor of the gallery.

"I didn't realize you would be here tonight, Mr. and Mrs. Jace," Sasha said.

"Jonathan hates to miss any of the Prescott George events, whether we're here or in London." The woman smiled lovingly at her husband, who glanced around the gallery as if displeased with the art there.

"You weren't here the night of Jordan's opening, so—"

"*That* wasn't a PG event." The old man practically snorted. "It was an art opening. Though my son uses the word quite loosely. Back in my day, art actually resembled something concrete. Didn't need the artist to spin a fanciful story to explain it."

Sasha pressed her lips together tightly and managed an obligatory smile, though her blood was boiling.

Did he have any idea what Jordan had achieved already in his short career as a sculpture artist? Or how many of his pieces stood in the courtyards of towns and corporate headquarters? How could the man be so flippant about such a remarkable achievement?

Jordan's parents were staying at their place in San Diego, and they'd managed to attend a Prescott George event at his gallery. Yet, they hadn't bothered to attend his opening.

*No wonder Jordan is so resentful and pretends not to care what they think.*

"Thankfully, not everyone is as stodgy and out-of-touch as you are, dear." Eva gave her husband a pointed gaze. "Whether you like it, or not, our son has made quite a splash in the art world. And Miss Charles here is going to help him gain the attention his work deserves."

"He gets plenty of attention, on the arm of one woman or another," he groused. "None of it good."

Sasha's cheeks flamed and her teeth clenched. Her stomach burned, thinking about some of the photos and articles she'd read. Instead, she focused on all of the wonderful things she knew about Jordan Jace. Things he'd kept from the world, and apparently, Eva and Jonathan Jace.

"We're working hard to change that, Mr. Jace."

"And exactly how is this little *project* going?" The man shoved a hand in his pocket. "You might as well know that I was against this little excursion. Enough time and money has been spent on Jordan's little hobby here." He gestured around the space. "What we should be doing is trying to talk him into making the sensible decision to join his brothers at Jace Investments."

*That. Was. It.* Sasha clenched her hands into fists at her sides.

"Mr. Jace, you have no idea just how much good your son has done in underserved communities here in San Diego. Not to mention the strong message his art sends about our need to be better stewards of the planet and our environment." Her voice vibrated with controlled anger. She should stop while she was ahead, but she couldn't. She had to defend him. "Perhaps his pieces aren't as literal as you'd like them to be, sir, but they're quite magnificent, if only you'd give them a chance."

Jonathan grunted. Though instead of anger there was something in his gaze that resembled admiration. It quickly faded, replaced by irritation. He folded his arms.

"I apologize if, at times, I seem a bit rough around the edges. But this is our son's future we're talking about here." He sighed, running a hand through his hair.

"I understand, Mr. Jace. But it is *Jordan's* future. Shouldn't he have a say in it?"

The man narrowed his gaze. "Maybe it makes me old-fashioned, but life was better in the old days. When sons eagerly followed their fathers into the family business. When art was art. And when Prescott George did things that truly mattered. Something more than milling around galleries comparing the size of our wallets and our overpriced collections of watercolor scribblings and leftover plane wreckage."

Jonathan Jace straightened his jacket and looked beyond Sasha at his wife. "I'm stepping out for some air."

Sasha slowly turned toward Mrs. Jace, her heart racing. She fully expected the woman to tell her she was fired for speaking to her husband that way. That she would see to it that Sasha never landed another worthwhile account in this town or anywhere else. What she saw instead stunned her.

Eva Jace's face was animated by a genuine smile. "Don't worry about my husband. His bark's far worse than his bite. Deep down, he's a cuddly teddy bear. If you can get past the spikes and barbed wire."

"I honestly didn't intend to upset Mr. Jace. But his perception of Jordan is so disparaging. I thought if only…" Sasha folded her hands, her eyes lowered. "I hoped I could give him a clearer picture of his son's accomplishments."

"Sounds like you're quite impressed with my son, Miss Charles. Enough to go to bat for him at your own peril."

Sasha's cheeks flamed with heat. Her eyes didn't quite meet the woman's.

*This is where I get shown the door, showered by bits of confetti that were once pieces of my contract. But it's too late to back down now.*

"Jordan is a remarkable artist, Mrs. Jace, and an extraordinary man. There's much more to him than meets the eye." She raised her gaze to Eva's. "And that's exactly what you hired me to demonstrate to the world."

"I knew you were the right woman for this job. That you'd be able to see through the silly facade

Jordan presents to the world." Eva squeezed Sasha's arm and gave her a grateful smile.

"I appreciate your confidence in me, Mrs. Jace. I won't let you or Jordan down. He's going to do incredible things in the future. I truly believe that."

"Yes, dear, I believe you do." The woman regarded her fondly. "Now, enough about my son for now, Miss Charles. Why don't you come sit down and tell me a little more about you?"

Jordan was sick to death of talking about the tomfoolery going on at Prescott George. First, Vaughn had practically accused him of being the culprit behind the break-ins and vandalism at the PG headquarters. Now they were behaving as if he had an obligation to help nail the childish bastards who'd pulled off the ridiculous prank.

Isn't that why they'd hired the blowhard, private detective currently giving them a rundown of what he'd uncovered? And what had the man learned for all of his overpriced investigations?

Jordan was temporarily distracted by thinking of countless adjectives to sum up exactly what this man had discovered thus far.

Sweet Fanny Adams. Damn all. Nix. Nada. Zilch.

He forced himself to focus on the conversation again. Jordan had promised Sasha that he would take his association with Prescott George more seriously. That he'd maximize his membership in the group, rather than treat it as a penance for his refusal to join his family's company.

He was all for making the membership work for him. However, Sasha had insisted that the only way to do that was to work harder to build relationships within the club. He was trying, he honestly was. Only, Vaughn Ellicott, Christopher Marland and a few of the other blokes at the club were making it quite difficult right now.

Jordan would much rather be out there in the gallery, entertaining Sasha Charles and rubbing elbows with potential buyers. Instead, he was huddled in his office for a ten-minute meeting that had ballooned to forty minutes and counting.

He checked his watch for what felt like the fiftieth time. Mercifully, Vaughn finally seemed to get the hint.

"We're not getting anywhere with this tonight, fellas." Vaughn climbed to his feet. "And my bride is out there wandering the gallery all alone, as are your significant others. So let's break it up and plan to chat about it again in a week or so."

*Goody.*

More hand-wringing, useless theories and long-winded debates that delivered exactly zero answers.

*Can't wait.*

But like the others, he mumbled his agreement. He'd have done just about anything, short of gnawing off his own leg, to escape the small space overloaded with testosterone, so he could spend some time with Sasha.

Jordan stepped out into the gallery, which buzzed with activity. Prescott George members, potential members and their guests had quickly filled the space. Chatter, laughter and music filled the air.

He scanned the main floor of the gallery. No sign of Sasha. His gaze met Lydia's and she smiled.

"Lyddie, has Sasha arrived yet?"

"Yes." Her smile stiffened. She sniffed and pushed her glasses further up on her nose. "She arrived about a half an hour ago."

His heart soared. "Where is she?"

"She went upstairs to talk with Mrs. Ellicott a while ago." Lydia indicated Vaughn's new wife, who was talking to a few other wives and significant others of PG members. "But Mrs. Ellicott came down about fifteen minutes ago."

"Is Sasha still upstairs?"

Lydia shrugged. "She must be. I haven't seen her down here."

"Thanks, Lydia." Jordan patted her shoulder and headed off to find Sasha, but she grabbed his elbow.

"I have three potential buyers who've been waiting to see you." Lydia leaned in closer, whispering just loud enough for Jordan to hear her. "That is the real point of this event, isn't it?"

"Yes, I s'pose it is." Jordan heaved a sigh and rubbed the back of his neck. "You always keep me on track. Thank you, Lyddie. Don't know what I'd do without you."

A reticent smile lit the woman's blue eyes. "Just doing my job."

"Jordan, you haven't seen my daughter Jojo, have you?" Chris Marland, president of the Prescott George San Diego Chapter, appeared beside him. The man's gaze swept the room.

"Not since we left the meeting." He'd met the girl and her brother when they'd arrived with their father earlier in the evening. "But if I see her, I'll let her know you're looking for her."

Jordan followed Lydia to the first of three members who were interested in either purchasing sculptures or having one commissioned.

When finally he'd met his obligation by talking to each of them, he bounded up the stairs in search of Sasha.

She was seated in a corner where his mother was speaking to her.

"Mother, what are you doing here?" He approached them, leaning down to allow his mother to kiss his cheek. "I didn't expect you here tonight."

"Your father and I arrived some time ago." His mother beamed at Sasha. "I've just been getting to know Miss Charles here a bit better. And she's been updating me on her progress." The corners of her mouth suddenly tugged downward and the light in her brown eyes dimmed. "Jordan, darling, why didn't you tell me about the work you've been doing with the schools? Or that you've been mentoring young artists?"

Jordan glanced quickly at Sasha, who gave him a reassuring nod, then back at his mother again.

He shrugged, sliding onto the sofa beside his mother. "Would it have mattered? If I'm interested in anything other than joining the family business, you and Dad have always turned a deaf ear. Why would this be any different?"

His mother was silent for a moment. She squeezed his hand.

"I'm sorry for that, Jordan. Not encouraging your interests is one of my biggest regrets. In fact, it's the primary reason I hired Miss Charles here." His mother gestured toward Sasha. "To show you how proud I am of what you've accomplished. And that I believe you're capable of achieving even more."

Jordan was stunned, rendered speechless for once in his life. He swallowed back the rising emotions caught in his throat.

His mum was actually apologizing. And was proud of what he'd accomplished.

"Thank you, Mum." He hugged her tight.

She cradled his cheek and smiled.

"Where's Dad?" he asked.

His mother glanced around. "He's wandering around here somewhere."

Jordan scanned the upper floor of the gallery. His

father was walking around one of his more daring pieces. A frown was plastered on the man's face.

Typical. Jordan honestly couldn't remember the last time he'd done anything that had impressed his father or earned anything more than a scowl.

"Dad obviously doesn't share your view." Jordan nodded toward his father who'd walked over to another piece.

His mother patted his knee. "He's always had a very specific plan for you. For all of you. He hasn't let go of that vision. And he's yet to understand what I learned here today."

Jordan studied his mother. "Which is?"

"That it doesn't reflect poorly on us as parents that you've gone your own way. It means we've done our job. Given you the strength and courage to follow your own path. Even if that means going against our wishes." She smiled broadly. "In that, you've been our biggest success yet."

"Thanks, Mum." His heart squeezed in his chest and he hugged her one more time. "That means a lot to me. It really does."

"To me, too." His mother stood and straightened her skirt. "Well, I'd better go join your father. I'll see you two later."

Jordan stood with his mother, taking a seat again when she walked away. He and Sasha remained silent for a moment. Finally, Jordan opened his mouth and turned to her.

She cut him off before he could speak.

"Before you say anything... I know it wasn't my place to tell your parents about the work you've been doing. But your father was going on about how your art wasn't real art, and I just couldn't let that stand."

Jordan raised a brow. "You had a row with my father over my work?"

Her cheeks flushed. "It wasn't really an argument, but yes, I did kind of tell him off. I know it wasn't the brightest move I've ever made, but I wasn't about to let him get away with—"

Jordan slid beside her on the sofa and pressed a finger to her lips in one fluid move. "I'm going to kiss you, Sasha Charles," he whispered, leaning in closer. "Any objections?"

Sasha stared at him, blinking rapidly. Her heart raced. She should reject his proposition and push him away. But she couldn't. Rooted in place, she slowly shook her head, eager for a taste of his mouth.

"Good." Jordan closed the remaining space between them, his lips nearly meeting hers.

"Jordan. There's something you need to see. Right away." It was Chris Marland. The man looked like he was completely out of breath, his chest heaving.

"We are going to finish this later." Jordan cupped her chin and sighed before turning to the chapter president. "What is so all-fired important that you need to disturb me at this particular moment?"

Chris hesitated. "One of the sculptures you've been working on…it's been vandalized."

"What?" He shot to his feet and Sasha stood beside him. His heart pounded. "Which one?"

"I don't know. There's no name on it. But I'd guess I'd say it resembles a bird."

Chris hadn't finished his sentence before Jordan hit the stairs, the sound of his own pulse filling his ears. He raced toward his studio.

He'd gone into the studio earlier, with the intention of returning straightaway. But he'd been distracted by the impromptu meeting being called, so he forgot to go back and lock it.

Jordan hadn't considered for one moment that someone might wander in there. Let alone someone who would sabotage his work.

He rushed through the crowd, briskly excusing himself. Finally, he reached the studio, where Vaughn Ellicott was already surveying the scene.

Jordan stopped dead in his tracks when he saw the damage to the sculpture. Someone had taken a pipe and repeatedly bashed the statue. Paint had been splashed onto the sculpture and formed little puddles all around it. A few of the containers that held bolts, screws and other smaller scraps of metal had been knocked to the floor.

His jaw tensed and his hands balled tightly into

fists. Jordan's body shook with the rage that spread through him. Like a toxin introduced intravenously.

Of all the pieces the saboteur could've attacked, he'd chosen that one. The piece that meant more to him than any damn thing he'd done in his entire career.

"Who could've done this?" Sasha's voice was behind him.

"Whoever's behind the break-ins at the Prescott George headquarters," Vaughn answered.

"You really think they would begin targeting the individual members of the club?" Chris asked.

"Not necessarily the individual members. This was about disrupting our event," Vaughn said definitively.

"Well, they've certainly achieved that." Chris stepped closer, assessing the mess. "And this doesn't bode well for any future events we have planned, like the Chapter of the Year event scheduled for next month."

Vaughn sighed heavily. "We're not looking much like a chapter to be emulated, are we? Especially if these acts are being perpetrated by one of our very own members."

Chris shook his head and sighed. "I'd better call the police."

"No." Jordan turned around, his eyes blazing. He bit back the anger rising in his chest.

*If not for the inane meeting Chris called, this*

*wouldn't have happened.* But there was nothing he could do about that now. So instead he'd focus on the big picture.

"I refuse to give them what they want." Jordan pointed at the vandalized sculpture. "I will not let them disrupt this event and make us all look like incompetent fools."

"We have to bring the police in." Chris's tone was quiet. Sympathetic.

"And we will." Jordan studied the mangled, paint-splattered sculpture. "*After* the event is over. I won't let these cowardly bastards win."

"Then we'd better get out of here and leave everything as we found it." Chris walked carefully toward the door and Vaughn followed him.

"You two coming?" Vaughn asked.

"We'll be along shortly," Sasha said, her voice soft.

"One more thing…" Jordan turned to Vaughn and Chris. "Who discovered this?"

"Your assistant Lydia said that she found the mess when she came in here to look for something," Chris said.

"Why didn't she tell me herself?"

Chris shrugged. "She seemed pretty shaken by the whole ordeal when she told me. Maybe she was nervous about how you'd react." He turned and left.

Jordan and Sasha stood in the large space he'd

brought her to the night they'd met. Neither of them spoke for several seconds.

"Look, I appreciate you being here." Jordan stared at the wreckage, trying to wrap his mind around how he'd go about salvaging the piece. "But I'd quite like to be alone."

Sasha didn't speak or move. Finally, she stepped closer and slipped her hand in his. "It's okay to need other people sometimes, you know. You don't always have to be the lone-wolf rebel."

Jordan's gaze snapped to hers. He'd wanted to yell and scream. To kick things over and bash the wall with a pipe. The kinds of things proper English gentlemen never did. The kinds of things they certainly never did before an audience.

He wanted to insist she leave and let him work out his anger in his own way. But the warmth and comfort there in her brown eyes stopped him cold. It soothed his wounded soul and lifted some of the anxiety that pressed down on him and made the taking of each breath laborious.

"Perhaps you're right." Jordan squeezed her hand back.

"We'd better join the others." She released his hand. "The party is in full swing."

"Shit."

"What is it?"

"As the host, I'm supposed to say a few words."

He checked his watch. "I'm scheduled to do that shortly."

"Do you think you can manage?" Sasha's voice was filled with concerned. "No one would blame you if you were too upset to talk right now. I'm sure one of the others would be glad to speak on your behalf."

"No, this is something I must do." His voice was more insistent. "I won't allow this coward to ruin my night. This event is part of the plan to help promote the gallery and my work. That's still the case."

They returned to the gallery, as if nothing had happened. But as Jordan surveyed the crowd, he couldn't help wondering if the culprit was among them. Perhaps even a fellow member of Prescott George.

## Chapter 8

Sasha hadn't been able to take her eyes off Jordan. She admired how he'd put on his best face and turned that brilliant smile up to its highest wattage.

Anyone who didn't know him well would never have suspected his heart was broken and that the smile he wore masked the pain underneath.

It felt odd to put herself in that category—as a person who knew Jordan well. Despite her insistence that they keep things professional, they'd grown closer in the weeks since she'd met him.

During their time together on the yacht, she'd learned to read his expressions and body language. She recognized when he was being honest and open—which was most of the time. But she'd also learned to recognize when he was masking some other feeling. Hurt, disappointment, anger...lust.

Sasha stood on the fringe of a small group of PG members and their significant others embroiled in a lively discussion. She'd tried to engage in the conversation, but her thoughts kept drifting back to Jordan.

She was concerned about him.

Sasha laughed along with everyone else in response to the story Vaughn and Miranda were telling of how they met. But all she could think about was how hard Jordan had taken the vandalism of the sculpture.

She could understand the anger. But there was something deeper there. Something he wasn't saying.

Sasha glanced over at Jordan. He was at the bar getting another drink. She wanted to go and comfort him. Hold him in her arms and tell him everything would be fine. Kiss him.

Warmth filled her body.

*You were actually going to let him kiss you. Right here in the gallery. In public.*

They'd been in an out-of-the-way corner of the gallery, on the upper floor. But it wasn't unthinkable that someone could've happened upon them. Someone like Eva or Jonathan Jace.

She'd already nearly blown it by telling Mr. Jace

about himself when he'd insulted Jordan's work. Kissing Jordan would have made her another of "those women" that his father had complained about earlier. One of the countless women Jordan had dated or been rumored to have dated.

Sasha liked Jordan, but getting involved with her client would bring her professionalism into question. And for what? To end up as fodder for the gossip blogs? She'd simply be another reject on the pile of Jordan Jace's discarded lovers.

*No thanks. I deserve more than that.*

That was the reason she'd turned down Jordan's proposal of a meaningless fling. It'd been a good decision then, and it was a good decision now.

*Don't let your libido and your heart do the thinking. Stay strong.*

Sasha was struck by those words. *Don't let...your heart do the thinking...*

Her attraction to Jordan wasn't just about desire and need. She genuinely felt something for him. More than she'd felt for any man in a very long time.

Warmth filled Sasha's cheeks. She glanced around, suddenly self-conscious. As if every other person in the room was privy to the lustful thoughts about Jordan Jace playing out in her head in vivid, HD color and earthshaking surround sound.

Miranda's gaze met hers and her friend furrowed her brow, her head cocked. As if questioning whether everything was all right. Sasha forced a smile, but Miranda seemed unconvinced. Fortunately, Vaughn drew Miranda back into the conversation before she could make her way over to Sasha.

Sasha released a quiet sigh.

She couldn't talk about Jordan's sculpture being vandalized, and she wasn't prepared to discuss the unsettling feelings she had for him.

Sasha glanced over at Jordan. He held court with a small group of people, regaling them with a fanciful interpretation of one of his pieces. The kind of flourish that apparently irked his father and made him long for the good old days. A sense of nostalgia Jonathan Jace and his son shared. Though their ideas about exactly what it was that made the good old days so good varied considerably.

On the outside, Jordan was all ease and joviality. But a hint of darkness in his eyes belied his exceedingly vivacious mood.

Sasha studied Jordan. The man was ridiculously handsome. His lean, muscular form, highlighted by the athletic cut of his suit, would rival any ancient Greek sculpture.

Fingers aching to trace the muscles of his arms and chest, Sasha's hands twitched at her side. She tried to stop imagining how incredible his body must look, underneath that suit.

She swallowed hard, gulped a fresh supply of air and tried to focus on what Vaughn was saying.

It was awful that Jordan's sculpture had been

damaged. But if Chris Marland hadn't interrupted them, she would've made a horrible mistake.

"Miss Charles." Eva Jace, suddenly by her side, placed a hand on her arm. "Can we talk for a moment?"

Sasha nearly jumped out of her skin. The woman was either a cat or an apparition, because Sasha could swear she hadn't been there a few seconds before.

And what more did Eva want to know?

The woman had already plied her with enough questions to make Sasha wonder if Jordan's mother intended to write her unauthorized biography.

"Of course, Mrs. Jace." She followed the woman to a quieter corner of the gallery.

"Jonathan and I are leaving shortly, but I need to ask a favor of you." The older woman lowered her voice and glanced around the room. "I'm worried about Jordan. Something's happened. I don't know what it is, but I noticed a change in his demeanor."

Sasha's spine stiffened. The members of the club had obviously wanted to keep what happened quiet. Particularly, while the event was going on.

"Really?" Not a lie, but not an admission, either.

"Come now, dear." Eva gave her a knowing smile. "I couldn't help noticing that you've kept a watchful eye on him all evening."

Sasha's mouth fell open. "I… I was just—"

The woman was nice enough to ignore her stammering.

"I know this isn't part of your job description, Miss Charles, but could you see to it that Jordan gets home safely this evening? I always worry about what he might do when he's like this."

"Oh, I don't know if I can—"

"The way Jordan talks about you…it's obvious he likes you very much. More importantly, he seems to trust you. More than he trusts or listens to his father or me these days." Her gaze drifted down to her hands for a moment, before meeting Sasha's gaze again. The corners of her eyes were damp. "I realize this is an inconvenience, so I'm willing to pay any extra fees."

The woman reached in her clutch and pulled out her checkbook.

"That won't be necessary." Sasha held up a hand, glancing over at Jordan momentarily. There was that look again. Like dark clouds gathering overhead. She turned back to Eva. "I'll make sure he's okay. I promise."

Eva clasped Sasha's arm. "Thank you."

Sasha sighed, rocking back on her heels.

Clients often made special requests. All things considered, a wealthy woman asking her to see to it that her grown son made it home without doing something stupid didn't even make the list of the top ten odd client requests.

But she hadn't felt anything for any of those clients. So this request felt very different.

Sasha avoided Miranda's inquisitive gaze and did her best to follow along in the conversation. After all, she was standing with a group of ultrawealthy, potential clients.

"There you are." Jordan approached her, excusing himself to Vaughn and Miranda before whisking her away to a quieter space. "I'm sorry we haven't had more time to chat this evening, but I know how important it is to you to avoid the perception that we're dating."

Jordan's eyes danced and one edge of his mouth curled in a smirk when he said the words. He studied her, awaiting her reaction.

"How thoughtful of you." Sasha kept her expression even. "Maybe I can return the favor. It's been a rough night for you, and you've had quite a bit to drink, so I'd like to take you home. To your home, of course." Her cheeks burned.

One brow lifted in amusement. "You're offering to escort me home personally, instead of calling for a car service?"

Sasha fought back the urge to tell Jordan that this wasn't her idea at all. That she was doing this at his mother's request. Only, there was a good chance Jordan would be upset by his mother's interference. After all, he'd often complained about his parents' need to control him.

He'd comply more easily if he believed it was her idea.

"Because it's the only way I can guarantee that my client goes straight home tonight, rather than doing something I'll be forced to clean up later."

"You sound like my mother."

Sasha pressed her lips into a straight line. "I sound like the woman charged with making sure the only press you get is good press. And, hopefully, I sound like a friend who's concerned."

"Why should you be concerned?" The corners of his mouth tugged down in a frown.

"You were really upset about your sculpture being damaged." She lowered her voice and glanced around, to ensure no one else was close enough to overhear them.

"I'm bloody furious. Someone entered my studio and vandalized my work. Haven't I a right to be upset?"

"Of course." She placed a gentle hand on his arm, her gaze meeting his. "But you don't just seem angry. You seem really...sad."

Jordan slipped his arm from her grip under the guise of shoving his hand in his pocket. He scanned the gallery, his eyes no longer meeting hers.

"If you insist, you may take me home. Perhaps you'll consider allowing me to repay your kindness with a nightcap."

"You've had quite a lot to drink already." Sasha frowned.

"Careful." He leaned in closer. "Now you're really beginning to sound like my mother."

"We'll see." Sasha huffed. Jordan seemed to need the company. "Find me when you're ready."

Sasha walked away, her heart beating wildly and her pulsing racing. She should be dreading the task of babysitting Jordan Jace.

Instead, she was eager to spend time alone with him.

The ride to Jordan's house in Coronado was quiet. The police weren't happy they'd waited to call, rather than calling as soon as they learned of the break-in. While most of the possible suspects were still on the premises.

There was practically steam coming out of Jordan's ears, and she'd never seen his jaw so tense and his face so stern.

"Jordan, I realize the officer didn't exactly have a warm-and-fuzzy demeanor, but he was only doing his job."

"Is that what you call doing his job?" Jordan's British accent had thickened. "Because it seems to me that part of his job is proper deportment with the citizens he's agreed to protect and serve. Instead, he behaved as if we'd disturbed him in the middle of a rather lovely bubble bath."

Sasha snorted with laughter at the image that popped into her head. The rotund, middle-age officer whose hairline had practically receded to the back of his neck. In a tub full of bubbles wearing a pink shower cap.

"You think that's funny?"

That only made her laugh more. She held up a hand. "I'm not laughing at you. Or the situation. It's serious. Of course. It's just…when you said the thing about him being in a bubble bath, a hilarious visual pinged in my head. The only thing that was missing was the yellow rubber ducky."

Now Jordan smiled slightly, too. He shook his head. "That isn't a very pretty picture at all, is it?"

They both laughed and the tension in Jordan's shoulders seemed to ease slightly.

"But seriously," he said, once he'd composed himself again. "The man was a knobhead. I didn't appreciate his not-so-subtle implication that I might have done this myself as part of some absurd insurance scam. Evidently, he doesn't understand that what makes that ragtag pile of scrap metal valuable is my ability to craft it into something more. How on earth would destroying it in process achieve that?"

"I know he came off a bit gruff, but he had to ask those questions."

"You're defending him?"

"Not exactly." She sighed, taking a turn down

his street. "But my grandfather was a beat cop most of his career. He was an honorable man who did his job, despite the nonsense he had to deal with in and out of the department. And when he retired, he started the security firm my father and brothers run now. So I try not to arrive at snap judgments."

"I didn't mean to imply that all officers are bad at their jobs," he said quickly. "But I wish that officer had your same policy of not jumping to conclusions. It wasn't only me he was accusing."

"I know." She nodded. "But his theory about you all suspecting that the culprit is a member of the club…he was right about that, wasn't he?"

Jordan didn't answer. He didn't need to. Of course, they would be reluctant to have that ugly fact revealed to the public. Particularly when their club was celebrating being named Chapter of the Year.

"Turn up this drive here."

"It's beautiful, Jordan." Sasha pulled into the narrow drive of the beautiful, contemporary glass-and-stucco home situated among palm trees. "And it fits you. It's like a piece of art."

"I'm glad you approve." A wide smile spread across Jordan's face. In any other instance, she'd have considered those words sarcastic. But his eyes and his tone were sincere. "I'd love to give you the grand tour. What do you say?"

Sasha stared longingly at the house. The architecture of the three-level home was breathtaking.

"The house is incredible, and I'd love to see it, but it's late. Perhaps another day?"

There was zero conviction in her tone. Even she recognized that. She desperately wanted a tour of Jordan's gorgeous home, and wasn't ready to say good-night.

"You said I seemed more than just angry about the sculpture that was damaged. You were right. The sculpture I was working on…it means more to me than anything I've ever done."

"Why?" She tried to read his eyes in the darkness between them.

"Come up for coffee and I'll explain." There was no levity or flirtatiousness in his voice. Just the voice of a man who needed to talk to a friend.

Sasha took a deep breath and nodded, ignoring all the signs that warned her not to step out of that car.

She barreled through every one of them and followed Jordan up the front steps of his impressive home. It wasn't a sprawling estate like the home her friend Miranda shared with her new husband, Vaughn. But what the home lacked in size, it more than made up for in style. The waterfront property offered stunning views of the San Diego skyline across the San Diego Bay.

Jordan gave her a tour of the space with its clean,

contemporary design. Floor-to-ceiling windows, two terraces and a patio kept the place open and airy. Sasha could only imagine how bright the space must be when the sun was out.

Much of the furniture was composed of stainless steel and glass which reflected the light. Abstract paintings and sculptures were featured throughout, complementing the artistic feel of the architecture.

"Your house is stunning, Jordan. Thank you for allowing me to see it." Sasha stood in the kitchen, complete with gleaming, professional grade, stainless steel appliances.

"Thank you." He handed her a fragrant cup of caramel vanilla coffee topped off with the creamer she'd requested. "I do love the house, but I purchased it for the view." He held up his coffee cup. "It's warm enough tonight. Why don't we have our coffee on the terrace so we can enjoy it?"

Sasha inhaled the aromatic coffee, then took a sip. A cup of coffee that delicious deserved to be savored over a beautiful view. "Lead the way."

Jordan and Sasha stepped out onto the second-floor terrace outside his living room.

The view overlooked the San Diego Bay. The San Diego skyline glittered like diamonds in the distance.

"The view was impressive from inside the house, but seeing it from out here…" Sasha put down her coffee and stood at the Plexiglas railing. "It honestly takes your breath away."

Jordan leaned against the wall, sipping his coffee as he studied Sasha in the moonlight.

He could easily say the same about her.

She was gorgeous in a sleeveless, plum-colored dress that hugged her vivacious curves like its very reason for being was to highlight Sasha Charles's God-given assets. Mile-high stilettos in an unexpected hue added a pop of color against the dark dress and her brown skin. And they made Sasha's lean legs appear to go on forever. Drawing his eye to the hem of her skirt, which fell just above her knee.

"It was this view that sealed the deal. I'd seen the house before, and I liked it well enough. But not enough to move on it. I kept thinking I might find something that suited me a bit better." Jordan stood beside her, taking in the lovely view of San Diego. "Then one night, my agent—a lovely woman who'd grown tired of showing me every house from here to La Jolla—insisted I meet her here one evening."

"You probably thought she was coming on to you." Sasha could barely hold back a grin.

"I did," he admitted, chuckling. "But that isn't the point. The point is she showed me this view, and immediately I knew, without equivocation, that this was the one. That I'd be happy here for many years to come. We signed the contract right here on this terrace."

"That's a great story." Sasha's eyes twinkled. "And I can't disagree with your choice." She sat at the table and crossed her legs, still staring out at the city skyline. "Do you use the terrace much?"

"I'm not here as often as I'd like, but when I'm home I spend a good deal of my time on this balcony or the one upstairs, off my bedroom."

Sasha looked away, as if his mention of the bedroom made her uncomfortable.

He couldn't deny that he now had visions in his head of exactly what he wished they were doing now. But he'd promised himself when he invited her in that he'd be well behaved. That he wouldn't make a play for her. Despite their near-kiss at the gallery.

"The terraces are my favorite place to take meals and exercise in the morning. Sometimes I come out here to sketch an idea for a sculpture or to just sit and think." He joined her at the table. "In fact, it was here one morning over coffee that I got the idea for the sculpture I'm currently working on. The one vandalized this evening."

"Tell me about the sculpture." Sasha raised her gaze to his again, her head tilted.

"It's a tribute to someone I loved very much and lost far too soon." He dropped his gaze to his hands, pressed to the table. "My twin sister."

"I didn't know you were a twin. I'm so sorry

about the loss of your sister, Jordan. How long ago did you lose her?"

"Nearly twenty years ago." He stared into the distance, his lungs suddenly burning. "And in nearly two decades, talking about her hasn't gotten any easier. Most likely because my family behaves as if Jeanette never existed. It's hard to get over what you barely even acknowledge."

"I can only imagine how painful it must be for all of you."

"I certainly couldn't tell by any of them." He stood, agitated, and gripped the railing, his back to Sasha. "Seems my entire family is content to pretend she never was." Jordan turned to face her. "But *I* can't forget. More importantly, I don't want her life to be forgotten."

"Tell me about your sister." She stood beside him at the railing, both of them staring across the bay, as if it was an act of solidarity. "What was she like?"

"She was sweet with a bubbly personality." He smiled painfully, a vision of his sister's smile filled his head. "But she could be determined. To the point of being stubborn." He bit back the emotion that clogged his throat as he met her gaze. "In some ways, you remind me of her. Of what she might've grown up to be."

"You think I'm stubborn?"

"You're rather determined. But that isn't necessarily a bad thing." He smiled. "When we were kids, it became painfully obvious to me that I wasn't meant for the family business. I was dreadful with numbers, but I was good with my hands. I could sketch and mold just about anything into little sculptures." He smiled wistfully. "Even then, my parents weren't very impressed by that. But my sister encouraged me. Always told me how clever I was to be able to do such a thing. That she envied my ability to make magic out of nothing. She believed I'd grow up and be an artist, even when we were as young as nine years old. She's the reason I've never given up on my art or given in to my family's demands."

"You were lucky to have her as your sister."

"I was. Jeanette wasn't just my sister. She was my best friend. The only one I've ever really had." He blew out a long breath. "So I'm determined to create a sculpture in her honor that will grace a public park. I hope it will make people happy long after I'm gone."

"What's your idea for the sculpture?"

There were few people he discussed a piece with before it was complete, unless it was commissioned. While the sculpture had been commissioned by the city, they'd given him free rein to create whatever he liked.

He blew out a long, painful breath. "Nothing that will resemble my sister in a literal sense. It will be reminiscent of the things I loved most about her, and I'm dedicating the public art piece to her memory."

"What prompted you to honor your sister with this sculpture?"

"I was sitting out here about a month ago when it struck me that when I'm gone, there'll be no one to remember her. Or to mourn the loss of what she might've brought to the world. I named my gallery after her, but that didn't seem like enough."

"I thought your sister's name was Jeanette?"

"*Sorella* means sister in Italian. We lost her in Italy while on holiday."

"Jordan, I can't tell you how sorry I am." When Sasha turned to him, her beautiful brown eyes welled with tears, and her voice trembled with emotion. She seemed to truly understand his sense of loss, and it touched her. "If you don't mind me asking, what happened to Jeanette? Was she ill?"

It'd been so long since he'd heard another person utter his twin sister's name.

"She drowned." He swallowed past the lump in his throat. His lungs were still on fire and acid burned in his gut. That day and the role he played in it forever etched in his mind.

Sasha slid her warm hand in his, threading their fingers. A lifeline he needed at a moment when he felt he was falling apart. Fury, sadness and regret had churned inside him all night, desperate for release. He'd tried to tamp down the bitter brew of emotions. Carrying on as if everything was fine, cocktail in hand. But the more he'd tried to pretend, the more agitated he became.

He'd been grateful for Sasha's small acts of kindness. Her ability to recognize his pain beneath his smiles and laughter. Her insistence in escorting him home. Agreeing to come in for coffee and be a listening ear. And now this.

Jordan gently squeezed her hand. Acknowledged the act and his appreciation for it without a word.

They stood in silence, her hand in his, staring at the city across the bay. Her silent comfort wrapped itself around him. Warmed the chill he felt inside. Made him feel whole again, if only for as long as they stood there together in silence.

"I'd better go." She turned to him, slipping her hand from his. "But thank you for the coffee and the tour of your lovely home."

"The pleasure was mine." Jordan shoved his hands in his pockets. "Thank you for the ride and the chat."

There was something in her eyes as they met his. She opened her mouth to say something, then shut it quickly, dropping her gaze.

"What is it, Sasha?" He should let it go. She'd decided against saying it. He should just leave it at that. But he couldn't. He needed to know.

Sasha inhaled a deep breath as if gathering her

nerve. She flattened her palms against his chest and rose on her toes to kiss him.

Jordan didn't fight the kiss or give in to it. His fingertips drifted to her sides as she pressed her soft, sweet lips to his. As the idea settled over both of them.

He needed to know that they weren't just swept up in the emotions of the moment. That neither of them would regret what was happening between them.

Sasha seemed to recognize his reluctance. She looped her arms around his neck, signaling the need for more contact.

Jordan wrapped his long arms around her waist and hauled her closer. He kissed her back, gliding his tongue along the crease between her lips.

She opened them to him, a soft murmur escaping her mouth as his tongue slid along hers.

Heat filled his body and his heart hammered against his chest as he claimed her mouth. From the moment he'd first laid eyes on Sasha, he couldn't stop imagining the taste of her full, sensuous lips. How it would feel to hold her in his arms.

He kissed her hard, his tongue delving deep as he swallowed the small murmurs of passion emanating from the back of her throat.

His hands glided down her back and cupped her round bottom. He pulled her as tightly against him as the laws of physics would allow. Still, he wanted more. Jordan fought the urge to tug that little dress higher so he could feel more of the creamy thighs he'd been dreaming about since the day she'd worn those little shorts on their second not-quite-a-date.

He found the strength to break their kiss, but not enough to break his contact with her warm skin. Jordan trailed kisses along her jaw and down her neck. Over her beautiful, bare shoulders.

"You know I want you, Sasha." He pressed a kiss to her ear. "But don't do this out of pity. I couldn't bear that. Not when I've looked forward to this for so long."

She trembled slightly. As if the reality of what was happening between them had finally dawned on her. She didn't respond.

Jordan slipped his hand beneath her jaw, lifting it gently, so their eyes met. "Whatever your answer, it's okay, love. I'll be disappointed, perhaps. But I'll get over it. There's always tomorrow."

Her chest rose and fell rapidly. She scanned his eyes as if she'd find the answer she sought in them.

"Earlier tonight…when we nearly kissed…" For the first time since he'd met Sasha Charles she seemed almost shy. Lowering her gaze to his mouth, she sank her teeth into her lower lip. "I wanted you to kiss me."

His body ached with need for this woman. His mother's meddling aside, something drew him to Sasha. Like opposite poles of a magnet attracting one another. Sasha, with her virtue, sensibility and need for order, was most definitely the North.

Jordan's hand glided down to her neck, his gaze dropped to her mouth. He was desperate to kiss her again. To learn every inch of her curvy frame. But he couldn't ignore the persistent voice in his head. The one that reminded him that he did indeed possess a bloody conscience. And he'd never be able to live with himself if he took advantage of Sasha's kindness.

He looped his arms around her waist and tugged her closer again. "Then you should know that if I kiss you again, I've no intention of stopping until I have you in my bed. And I have every intention of making you mine tonight."

A small frown furrowed her brows when he said "tonight." She glanced out onto the water as if debating his terms of engagement in that beautiful head of hers.

Sasha had made it clear she wanted a relationship. One that could lead to love, perhaps even marriage.

That was more than he could offer.

He'd been up-front about that, and his position hadn't changed. Perhaps he hadn't met his parents' expectations of a proper English gentleman. But he wasn't a scoundrel who'd say or do anything just to have a romp with a beautiful woman. Especially one as sweet and kind as Sasha.

Not even if it meant his night would end in bitter disappointment.

"I know you want something more serious." For the first time, the words felt like an apology. "But I can't give you that. So, if you—"

Sasha pressed her open mouth to his again, cutting him off. She seemed intent on shutting his gob before he could talk her out of what she'd obviously decided.

His tongue crashed against hers. Lowering his hands to her full bottom, he pulled her soft, feminine body against his hardened knob. Made his intentions for the evening crystal clear. In case she'd chosen to ignore his earlier words.

He kissed her until they were both breathless and frustrated by the need for skin-to-skin contact.

Jordan forced himself to pull his mouth away, his chest heaving. He glanced around at the nearby homes. They'd already given his neighbors quite a show. It was time they moved inside.

Jordan gripped her hand and led her inside and up to his master suite, dimly lit by a bedside lamp. He moved to kiss her, but she turned around.

"Unzip me?"

Jordan slowly tugged the zipper down between her shoulder blades to the curve of her bottom. She shimmied out of the dress.

The lacy band of her thong was her only visible

covering. Her perfect, round bottom was even more glorious than he'd imagined.

When she turned around, it was evident that a bra had been built into the dress. Because he was greeted by brown, pebbled peaks, straining for his attention.

Jordan gripped her waist and hauled her against him, kissing her neck and shoulders. His kisses trailed down her chest until he found one of the hardened peaks with his mouth. Laved it with his tongue. Grazed it with his teeth. Then he gripped the round globe in his hand and sucked.

"Jordan." She braced his shoulders as she whispered his name. Made soft, approving murmurs that went straight to his bollocks. Ratcheted up his need for her to a full-blown inferno.

He moved to the other peak, lavishing it with the same treatment. Then he lifted her onto the bed and gently laid her back. He trailed kisses down her trembling belly, then along the band of the lacy thong.

He kissed his way down the silky fabric, then pressed a kiss on her most delicate flesh through the damp fabric covering it. She squirmed, but allowed her legs to fall open wider.

Jordan smiled as he pressed another kiss there. Then he trailed kisses up her inner thigh. Kissed the back of her knee before tracing the flesh with his tongue.

She tensed, a small gasp escaping her mouth.

*Good.* She anticipated what came next. That he'd taste her there until he got his fill of her. Until she could no longer stand it.

Jordan tugged aside the damp fabric. Pressed one kiss to her slick, swollen flesh. Then another and another. He glided his tongue along her glistening, pink slit. Relished her salty taste before spreading the flesh and diving his tongue inside her.

Sasha tensed, her heels driving into the mattress. She gripped the bedding, as if trying to control her reaction.

"Look at me, Sasha." He pressed soft little kisses to her flesh until she met his gaze. "It's okay, darling. You don't need to hold back with me." He pressed another louder, more intense kiss to the hardened nub between her legs.

She screwed her eyes shut, her head lolling back. "Oh God, Jordan. That feels so good."

"That's exactly what I want. To make you feel better than you've ever felt before."

She dug her heels into the mattress and slipped her fingers into his hair, tugging his mouth closer. Angling his head to exactly where she needed him.

Her hips moved against his mouth and she repeated a chorus of yeses and "Oh Gods" until finally she called his name. Her belly tensed and her inner walls convulsed.

Watching Sasha fall apart, his name on her lips,

was a thing of incredible beauty. One he wanted to experience again, this time plunged so deeply inside her that they'd barely realize where one of them ended and the other began.

He rose from his knees and retrieved a foil packet from his bedside table. Jordan undressed and sheathed himself, then joined her beneath the covers.

Sasha's soft gaze met his. She cupped his cheek and pressed a kiss to his lips. And he felt…something. Something he hadn't felt since he was a bumbling teenager, head over heels about his first real girlfriend.

The feeling was exhilarating and comforting, yet disconcerting. Because this wasn't about love. They were simply two people responding to a persistent desire. Filling a common need.

Jordan shook off the thought, hovered over her and pressed the head of his knob to her entrance. He concentrated on the inhalation of her breath and her sensual murmur as he slowly entered her. Until he was fully seated, his width stretching her.

He kissed her again, his tongue seeking hers as he rocked inside of her.

Sasha dug her fingers into his back, then gripped his arse, pulling him in harder and deeper.

He moved inside her, both of them damp with sweat, until her body stiffened and she clutched his shoulders. She called his name as she reached her peak again. Her walls spasmed around his heated flesh. Heightened the intensity of his arousal. His mouth pressed to her ear, he whispered all of the dirty things he had in store for her.

The sensation built with each movement of his hips, with each soft whimper coming from her sexy, little mouth. He cursed, his body stiffening as pleasure rolled through him like a freight train.

Jordan released a long, shaky breath as he collapsed into a sweaty heap beside her. He wrapped his arms around Sasha and pulled her to him.

He didn't want to think about the look he'd seen in her eyes. Or the feeling it triggered deep in his chest. He would enjoy the intimacy they'd shared and ignore the niggling feeling that, after tonight, neither of them would be the same.

# Chapter 9

Sasha awoke surrounded by warm skin and a solid male chest. Her eyes shot open and she blinked, adjusting to the unfamiliar space.

Jordan had one arm thrown over her waist. The other was pinned beneath her. And they were both completely naked.

Her heartbeat raced.

*What have I done?*

She breathed quietly, her eyes closed against the morning sunlight creeping through the wide expanse of windows on two sides of the space.

*You slept with your client, that's what you've done, genius.*

Even now, her body tingled from the memory of Jordan's skillful touch. Their night together had been incredible.

She was by no means virginal. But no man had ever given her such indescribable pleasure. Or made her feel the way she had when she'd looked in his eyes.

Until last night, Sasha had never slept with a man she wasn't in a relationship with. And yet, the emotions that swept through her, as she and Jordan made love, were deeper than anything she'd felt during her two-year relationship with a man she'd been sure she was going to marry.

*How could that be?*

She sighed softly. Jordan couldn't have been more wrong about her being with him out of pity.

Yes, she'd been moved by Jordan's loss and his decision to dedicate a public art sculpture to his sister. But she hadn't kissed Jordan because she felt sorry for him.

When he'd opened up to her and revealed his heart, she'd felt an intense connection to this complicated man. In that moment, she'd stopped fighting her desire to be with him.

Maybe she had been motivated by the need to comfort him. But what they'd shared had soothed something deep inside of her, too.

The toe-curling pleasure was a happy bonus.

But in the morning light, faced with the reality

of what she'd done, a growing sense of panic filled her chest. The strong arms that made her feel safe and warm throughout the night, suddenly felt heavy. Suffocating.

She needed air and space.

Sasha gently removed the arm draped over her body, careful not to wake him. She wasn't prepared to deal with the awkwardness of the morning after.

Sitting up slowly, quietly, she clutched the sheets to her chest. She glanced back at his sleeping form.

God, he was beautiful. His broad chest, covered with a smattering of hair, rippled with muscles. The sheet was slung low over his waist, allowing her gaze to follow the trail of hair that disappeared beneath it.

Sasha bit her lower lip and groaned silently, her nipples beading and the space between her thighs growing damp. She shut her eyes against the vision of how he looked, towering above her, as he made love to her.

A shiver ran down her spine and her hands trembled slightly. She needed to get out of there and go home. Take a shower, get changed and go about her day. As if this never happened. Jordan had made it clear that this meant nothing to him. Why couldn't she take the same approach?

*Because it did mean something to you.*

Sasha clenched her teeth and ignored the little voice in her head that chose *now* to give her a much-needed dose of reality. Her faulty, internal alert system was as useful as a passenger who warned of an impending collision *after* the vehicle was already wrapped around a tree.

She slipped from beneath the sheet, found her clothing scattered on his bedroom floor and slipped into the bathroom.

Her image, reflected in the mirror, condemned her for breaking her most important business and dating rules. Don't date clients and don't get involved with anyone who isn't serious.

Sasha showered, got dressed and hoped to hell Jordan would still be asleep when she left.

Jordan blinked against the sunlight spilling through the blinds in his bedroom. He usually closed the motorized, blackout shades before going to bed. But last night, he'd wanted to see Sasha in the moonlight.

*Sasha.*

He'd fallen asleep with her in his arms. Something he usually avoided, even on the rare occasions that he slept over at someone's place or allowed them to sleep over at his.

He reached for her, but she was gone.

Jordan propped himself up on his elbows and scanned the room. She wasn't there and the bathroom door was open. He called to her, but there was no answer.

Jordan pulled on a pair of boxers. He checked the terrace and the rest of the house, but Sasha wasn't there.

He yawned and made his way to the kitchen. There was a note on the counter.

Jordan,
Had to leave early for work. Last night was amazing. Thank you for a great night.
Sasha

Jordan ran a hand through his hair and huffed. *Why would she leave without saying goodbye?*

Because Sasha's note sounded suspiciously like a kiss-off. Translation: *Thanks, but no thanks. I've no intention of doing this again.*

Jordan checked his watch and groaned. He'd slept late. Perhaps Sasha slipped out because it was early and she hadn't wanted to wake him. Still, she should've said goodbye.

Even he had the decency not to creep out without saying goodbye.

Jordan made himself a cup of black coffee, stewing over Sasha's cryptic note.

He grabbed his coffee cup, found his mobile and rang her.

She didn't answer.

He waited a few minutes and rang her again as he searched his closet for something to wear to the studio. He'd be working late into the night to fix what damage he could and start over with any pieces that had been ruined.

"Good morning, Jordan." Her voice was tentative.

"I rather hoped we'd be having this conversation in person. There's nothing more awkward than the morning-after conversation by mobile. Except, perhaps, the morning-after conversation by text."

He'd hoped to lighten the mood with a little levity. But Sasha didn't laugh. And there was no indication of a smile in her voice.

"Sorry, I had to get into work early today." She sounded formal. Like they were complete strangers. Not like he was a man who knew her taste and had memorized her every curve.

"I can appreciate that, but I still wish you'd awakened me this morning." He smiled. "I had a very special goodbye planned."

She was silent for a moment too long. "Look, Jordan, last night was…amazing." Her voice was hushed. "But we both know it can't happen again. Not if we plan to keep working together."

"Why not? We're both adults with a clear understanding of the situation." He paced inside the closet. "Surely, we're both sensible enough to manage a business connection and a personal connection."

Her silence said she didn't agree. "I know, in theory, it seems possible. And maybe I'm just not mature or cosmopolitan enough. But I don't think I can manage both."

"Don't I get a choice as to which is more important to me?" He gritted the words through his teeth.

It was a cruel thing to say, he knew. They'd already discussed all the reasons his account was so important to her. Still, it wounded his pride to think she'd chosen her work over what they'd shared last night. As if it had meant nothing to her.

The irony of his inability to accept being on the wrong side of the awkward morning-after call wasn't lost on him.

The cosmos was having a great laugh at his expense. He deserved it, he was sure. But the fact that he had it coming didn't make getting kicked in the teeth hurt any less.

"I don't think we should see each other again casually. Period." Her words felt like the steel doors of a lift shutting in his face. "And if you don't think you can keep working with me, I respect that. I can recommend a few other highly qualified consultants here in our office."

"Sasha, there's no need to take such drastic measures." If he could just reason with her. Make her see how crazy it was to think that they couldn't be lovers and business associates. And perhaps even friends.

"Jordan, I'm sorry. I really am. I know better and I've never done this before. Never even been tempted to, I swear. So, no, I don't know how to deal with this."

His mobile alerted him to another call. It was

Lydia at the gallery. Jordan checked his watch again.

"That's Lydia calling. I have a meeting scheduled at the gallery this morning."

"Then you should go." Sasha sounded relieved.

"I'll ring her later. See if she can reschedule."

"No." Her voice was insistent. "The meeting sounds important. We can talk later."

"I'm going to hold you to that."

"Have a good day, Jordan." She didn't acknowledge his words. "Thank you again for last night. For telling me about Jeanette. It meant a lot that you trusted me with your memories of your sister."

*Hell of a way to repay that trust.*

"We will talk later." Jordan sighed, squeezing his eyes shut when Sasha ended the call without agreeing.

He'd missed Lydia's call, so he rang her up at the gallery and promised to be there as soon as he could take a shower and grab a bite to eat.

He tossed his phone on the bed, hoping the situation with Sasha would improve. After having her in his bed, all he could think of was having her there again.

Sasha exited the supply closet where she'd retreated to take Jordan's call. If she hadn't answered, he would've called again. Perhaps shown up in her office.

So she'd slipped into the closet like she did when she was thirteen, and her father thought she was too young to take calls from boys. Not a good look for a woman who was three years shy of thirty.

She shook her head, disgusted with her lack of judgment.

*What did you think would happen if you slept with him?*

But she hadn't been thinking last night. She'd only been feeling and wanting. And look at the mess she'd made.

Jordan Jace was no stranger to short-term dalliances. Once he got over his hurt pride, he'd see that she was right. Being lovers was a colossally bad idea.

"Got a call for you," her assistant, Melanie, mouthed.

"Who is it?" she mouthed back.

Melanie covered the phone and whispered, "Mrs. Jace."

Sasha froze, her muscles tensing and her heart racing.

Melanie raised an eyebrow and tilted her head. A knowing smile curled the edges of her mouth. She put the woman on hold on the pretense of going to find her.

"So, do you want me to put the call through to your future mother-in-law or what?"

Sasha's cheeks and forehead burned with heat.

"Oh. My. God. That's why you came tipping in here this morning acting all weird. You were with Jordan Jace last night, weren't you?"

Sasha shushed the woman, who couldn't stop grinning.

"I don't want to talk about last night," Sasha said in as serious a voice as she could muster.

"Okay, fine. We won't talk about whatever obviously did happen between you two last night." Melanie grinned, unable to hide her amusement over the boss behaving badly. "But Mrs. Jace is pretty persistent. If I put her off now, you know she's just going to keep calling."

*Like mother, like son.*

"Fine. Just give me a minute, will you? Then transfer her to my desk." Sasha went into her office and closed the door. She took a couple of deep, cleansing breaths before sinking into the chair behind her desk.

Melanie made eye contact with her through the glass partition. Sasha nodded that it was okay to put the woman through.

"Mrs. Jace. How can I help you this morning?"

"I wanted to see if you were able to get my son to go straight home."

"Yes. Yes, I was." Sasha tried to rid her mind of the images of last night. She could only imagine Mrs. Jace's reaction if she knew what had happened between her and Jordan last night. "He's fine. Really. I don't think you need to worry about him."

His mother sighed in relief. "I knew you'd handle it. You're as good as advertised, Miss Charles."

"Any member of our consultant team would've done the same." Sasha tried to sound cheery and upbeat.

"I'm sure they would've, dear," Mrs. Jace said. "But your firm wasn't recommended to me. It was your name I kept hearing from friends. And it was your results I was so impressed with. If you ask me, you're the crown jewel of that firm. They should be glad to have you."

"Thank you, Mrs. Jace. That's very kind. But something unexpected has come up. I might have to step away from Jordan's account and allow another member of our team to handle it. He'll be in just as capable hands, I assure you."

"I don't want hands that are just as capable. I want yours. Maybe you don't realize it, but you've already done wonders for my son. I've seen a great improvement in his website and social media. And the media page on his website looks impressive."

"And whoever takes over the account would simply execute the plan and strategies Jordan and I have already identified. The changeover would be seamless."

"I don't doubt that the plan would be the same." It was obvious the woman—who probably wasn't accustomed to being told no—was trying her best to remain calm. "But Jordan wouldn't be. He needs *you*. You're tough with him, but you're also extremely passionate about his work. You respect him. See the greatness in him. So, I beg to differ. Plugging someone else in your place will not be the same. Please reconsider, I beg of you. If money is the issue, we can renegotiate your fee."

"It isn't the money—"

"Let me talk to her." Mr. Jace was in the background. He'd never been a fan of her or spending money on her services. He'd be glad to call off the entire project.

"Miss Charles, this is Jonathan Jace."

"Yes, sir."

He sighed noisily, then was quiet so long she nearly thought the call had dropped.

"Please don't abandon my son now." His tone was very different than it'd been that night at the gallery. "Eva's right. You are good for Jordan. But you've been good for us, too. Me especially."

"I don't understand."

"You stood up to me the other day. Defended my son and his work. You made me rethink things. I was being unfair to Jordan. You made me see that. The boy has talent."

Sasha was too stunned to speak, so he continued.

"I know I can be gruff, at times. It isn't intentional. It's the way I was raised. I simply want the best for my children. And to leave my legacy to them. To all of them. But I realize now that isn't the best use of Jordan's talents. And I have you to thank for that. So please, Miss Charles, don't leave the job undone. Our boy needs you, and so it appears, do we."

"Mr. Jace, I don't know what to say."

"Say you'll stay on, dear." Mrs. Jace's voice was distant, but she apparently took the phone back from her husband. "You don't have to answer me now, but please, think about it. Even if you won't do it for us, think of all the additional business Jace Investments and our friends could throw your way, Miss Charles. This can be a long and lucrative relationship."

They were dangling an irresistible prize in front of her. One she couldn't, as a potential partner at the firm, turn down in good conscience.

She'd be throwing away what might be millions of dollars' worth of business because she hadn't had enough self-control to keep her hands to herself. And now she'd be compounding that by allowing her personal feelings to get in the way of business.

"I'll make arrangements, so I can stay on Jordan's account."

"Thank you, Miss Charles. I know you're quite busy, so we won't take up any more of your time."

Sasha hung up the phone and rested her head on the desk atop her folded arms.

She'd have to navigate the treacherous path she'd created for herself. That meant convincing Jordan Jace it would be better if they returned to a strictly professional relationship.

But first, she needed to convince herself.

# *Chapter 10*

Jordan stood and stretched, thankful that the meeting with Vaughn Ellicott, Chris Marland and a few other members of Prescott George had finally ended.

He and Marcus, his studio assistant, had spent the previous day cleaning the paint off the vandalized pieces of metal. They salvaged most of them, since they were just a little banged up. Then he and Marcus reassembled the previously finished parts of the sculpture.

Today, he didn't have Marcus's help, and business in the gallery had sidetracked him from his studio work. Then there was the Prescott George meeting.

He'd been tempted to blow the meeting off. But he'd taken Sasha's advice to heart. He was trying his best to take his duties at the club more seriously. That included his role as the community outreach liaison.

"We're headed out, and I'm going to lock up since no one else is here." Chris glanced down at his watch impatiently after Vaughn left.

"Actually, I plan to spend about an hour in my office here. I need to pull some info together for a community outreach project I'm considering," Jordan said.

Chris's eyes widened, as if Jordan had said he could fly or the sky was green.

The man's disbelief was warranted.

Jordan's appointment as the club's community outreach liaison had been purely political. Likely at his father's request. Jordan had accepted the position to pacify his father by giving the semblance of finally taking his membership seriously.

He'd been in his PG office a handful of times in the months since he'd agreed to accept the role.

It wasn't that Jordan didn't think the position was important. It was his disdain for the club and what it stood for. But Sasha had shown him how he could use the club to do more good than he ever could alone.

"I am still PG San Diego's community outreach liaison, aren't I?"

Chris nodded dumbly. "Yes, of course."

"Then I'll lock up when I'm done." Jordan dangled his key chain, then turned the corner toward his office.

A familiar voice drew Jordan's attention, stopping him cold.

"Chris Marland, right? You might remember me from the PG event at Sorella the other night."

*Sasha.*

Jordan turned back toward Chris, who stood at the end of the hall.

"Of course." Chris folded his arms, one brow raised. "You're Jordan's…consultant."

"I thought I might find him here."

"Right over there." Chris pointed in his direction.

Sasha rounded the corner, halting abruptly once she saw him. She thanked Chris, but didn't take any additional steps toward him.

Chris shook his head and left, no doubt believing that meeting Sasha was his real objective in staying.

Well, to hell with him. Chris could believe anything he wanted. He didn't need to jump through hoops to impress Christopher Marland or anyone else at the club.

"Did I interrupt something?" Sasha looked confused.

"No, he's just a perpetual grouch. Come on in." Jordan beckoned her, only half joking. No need to upset her with what Chris likely thought. After all, that wouldn't help his argument. "I was just heading to my office."

He unlocked the door and let her in, surveying the space.

"This is my first time here," Sasha said suddenly, as if she desperately needed to say something. Anything. "It's a lovely building. This is the old brewery, right?"

"So they tell me." He tried not to show his amusement. "Have a seat, please."

She nodded and sat in the chair. Neither of them spoke for a moment. Finally, she stopped surveying the room long enough to look at him.

"I'm sorry I didn't call first. But I've been trying to reach you since yesterday. I couldn't leave a message because your voice mail is full. And you didn't answer today, either."

"And how'd you know I was here?"

"Lydia mentioned that you were unreachable because you were in a meeting here at the Prescott George offices. I'm sure she meant to get rid of me, but I took a chance on catching up with you here once the meeting ended."

"Then it must be pretty important." He settled back in his chair, studying her face.

"It is."

The last time a woman tried this hard to reach him was his first and last pregnancy scare when he was barely twenty. Thankfully, it'd been a false alarm. "I'm all ears."

"I need to tell you I'm sorry about the other night. It was all my fault. I shouldn't have kissed you. *I* insisted we keep the relationship strictly business. Then I failed to keep my end of the bargain."

"So you're here to tell me you wish you hadn't slept with me. Well, that wouldn't crush a fellow's ego, now, would it?"

"I didn't mean it that way." Sasha winced, pressing a hand to her forehead. "It was great. You know that. The quality of the encounter is not the issue. It's that it should never have happened at all. Because you're my client and I'm bound by a code of ethics. And I failed it miserably."

Jordan clenched his teeth, trying not to be incredibly insulted. It was as effective as a rubber band trying to stop a speeding train.

"All right, Miss Charles." He grinned slyly when she narrowed her gaze at his use of formal address. "We screwed up. Both figuratively and literally. So now what?"

"If you're agreeable to it, I'd like to continue as your brand strategist. But this time I'll keep my hands to myself."

Jordan crossed one leg over the other and stared at her for a moment, sizing her up. The guilt vibrated off her, as did the attraction between them.

"All right, Miss Charles, if you insist upon it, it

shall be so." He leaned forward in his chair. "Will that be all? Because I actually do have work to do here. I'm taking your advice and tailoring a program for the chapter."

"Jordan, that's wonderful." Her eyes danced with excitement. She seemed relieved that the conversation had shifted to business. "What do you have in mind?"

"Not surprisingly, something related to art, but I'm not sure what I want to do, yet. And I don't want to do anything stuffy or typical. It has to be something fun that will energize both old and new members as well as the community."

"That sounds good. If you want to do something different, then start by learning what the chapter has done in the past."

"The archives are located in the library. The last community liaison mentioned that there are photos in there documenting past events." He stood. "I'm going to have a look. Are you coming along or do you have to go now?"

She glanced at her watch. "I don't have to go, but maybe I should."

"I could use your help going through the archives." He smiled. "And, if you're up for it afterward, let me treat you to a late lunch." He held up his hand. "And no, it's not a date. It's a working lunch to flesh out some of my ideas."

Sasha nodded reluctantly, but followed him to the library.

They went through several albums of photos in the archives. Some of them dated back to the earliest days of the club. Jordan thought of his father's words when he was appointed the position.

*It's an important job, son. Assign it the importance it deserves.*

He hadn't done that. Instead he'd behaved as if he were a brooding child. But it wasn't his father or the club he'd been punishing. It was the members of disadvantaged communities who needed their help. Thankfully, the club participated in several ongoing community projects, arranged by previous liaisons. But now he had the opportunity to put his mark on the chapter and the community with a project of his own design.

"Jordan, what's the matter?" Sasha frowned. She was sitting on the floor, her legs folded beneath her as she reviewed some of the photos and made notes.

"Nothing." He put back one of the albums and sighed. He was thirty years old and still playing the part of the rebellious teen. No wonder his father was so disappointed.

Sasha's hand was on his forearm. "Are you sure you're all right?"

He'd been so deep in thought he hadn't seen her get up and walk over to the bookcase. But now he was very aware of her. Her scent and her warmth. The comfort he felt at the touch of her hand.

"I'm fine. Really." He slipped his arm from beneath her hand and shoved his hands in his pockets.

She stared at him, her arms folded and one hip cocked. The same hip bone he'd trailed kisses along just two nights ago.

He swallowed past the lump in his throat, his heart racing and heat building in his chest.

For the past hour, he'd been careful to keep his distance. To only talk about business. But here she was, invading his space and reminding him of all the things he loved about her.

"Let's make a deal," she said, her arms still folded. "This is a business relationship, but I don't see why it can't be a friendship, too. So if something is wrong, I want you to feel comfortable talking to me about it."

"Well, you really can't have everything you want, now, can you?" He raised his voice in frustration, and immediately regretted it. "Sorry. I didn't mean to sound cross, but I'm just a little…"

"Angry?"

"Yes. And frustrated and disappointed. Not with you, but with myself." He raked a hand through his hair and sighed.

She stepped closer. "Why are you angry with yourself?"

"Because for the first time I clearly recognize

what a tosser I've been with my parents. My dad, in particular. Yes, I had good reason to be angry with them, but I haven't handled it very well, have I?"

Sasha didn't answer.

She wouldn't lie to him. It was one of the things he loved about her.

"Sure, there are things you could've handled better. Like your responsibilities here at the club. Your father rejected your art. The thing you identified with most. It felt like a personal rejection. So you retaliated by rejecting the things he identified with—Jace Investments and Prescott George. I'm not saying I agree with how you handled it, but I do understand why you lashed out." A warm smile lit her eyes. "The important thing is you both recognize your mistakes now, and you're trying to change course."

"You're right, of course. But next time, won't you at least pretend to give me a little resistance when I'm down on myself."

They both laughed, and for a moment all of the awkwardness between them dissipated like storm clouds after the rain.

"Thank you, Sasha."

"For helping with the project?"

"For being a good friend. Even when I didn't deserve it." He forced an apologetic smile. "I didn't get to thank you properly for being there for me the other night."

"It was my pleasure, Jordan." She held his gaze, her eyes sincere. They stood in silence for a moment before she turned to walk away.

He caught her elbow, and when she turned back toward him, her lips parted and her gaze softened. Her cheeks were flushed.

Jordan leaned in, his mouth hovering over hers. Sasha lifted onto her toes and closed the distance between them. She pressed her open mouth to his and her palms to his chest.

He palmed her bottom, pulling her tight against him, hungry for the feel of her and the warmth of her skin.

Jordan savored the sweet taste of her mouth as his tongue glided along hers. He slid his hand down her thigh and wrapped her leg around him as he pressed her against the wall. She groaned when he lifted her higher and ground his hardened length against the apex of her thighs.

"God, I want you. Here. Now." She breathed the words in his ear. "Please."

There was no one there but them and no cameras in the space. And he wanted her, too. He removed his break-glass-in-case-of-emergency-only foil packet from his wallet and unzipped his trousers, freeing his member and sheathing himself.

He shoved her soaked panties aside and plunged his length inside her. Both of them groaned in relief at the sensation of their connection.

Jordan slipped his arms beneath both legs and gripped her waist. He lifted and lowered her onto him.

Both of them cursed and moaned. Beads of sweat formed on his brow from the effort. She braced her hands on his shoulders and pressed her back into the wall, taking him deep.

Finally, she called his name, her body trembling as her walls spasmed around his throbbing flesh.

He'd be content forever to watch Sasha come apart in his arms. To hear her calling his name, her voice strained and quaking.

Soon after, he was at the edge. Tumbling and crashing, his body quivering with the aftershocks of his orgasm.

He held her, both of them gasping for breath, their hearts racing. Jordan was reluctant to separate himself from her. But he had no choice.

Slowly, he set her on her feet. "I'd better go… you know."

"Me, too." She straightened her skirt and combed her fingers through her short curls. "Where's the ladies' room?"

"It's a men's club. So…" He shrugged and they both laughed, allaying some of the awkwardness they might have otherwise felt. "But there's a single bathroom just outside that door. I'll go to another and meet you back here in a bit."

She nodded, grabbed her purse and went outside. He waited a moment, then headed to another bathroom.

When she met him back in the library, they both started to speak all at once.

"You go first." She nodded toward him.

"Look, Sasha, I enjoy being with you. And I'm not just talking about the sex. I'm talking about the moments we've spent together over dinner or a movie. The conversations that make me feel like I've known you my entire life." He sighed, shaking his head. "I don't know what to call what we have. I only know that being with you is amazing, and I don't want to stop."

Sasha chewed her lower lip and raised her eyes to his. "I enjoy being with you, too. And despite the fact that this breaks nearly every one of my rules… I don't want to stop, either."

Jordan hugged her to his chest, sighing in relief, then he kissed her. "Give me a second to put everything away and I'll take you to lunch like I promised."

"One thing, though…as far as the world is concerned, we're just friends." She pressed a gentle hand to his chest when he opened his mouth to object. "I have to protect both my reputation and that of the firm's. Maybe it'd be different if we were an actual couple. But friends who are hooking up? I can't risk what it might do to our firm."

Jordan released a frustrated sigh. "If you think it best."

"I do." She stood on her toes and kissed him. "Thank you for understanding."

Jordan gritted his teeth and forced a smile. He'd been reduced to the relationship equivalent of dirty laundry. But as long as Sasha was going to be in his bed tonight, he'd learn to deal with it.

# Chapter 11

It'd been more than a week since he and Sasha had reached their agreement to keep seeing each other discreetly. He'd happily entertained her at his home most nights since then.

Jordan and Marcus had rectified nearly all of the damage caused by the still-unknown vandal. And they'd spent long hours working in the studio on the sculpture that was a tribute to his sister. He'd made a few amendments to the original plan. But even with all of that, they were still nearly on schedule.

Lydia knocked at the studio door before coming inside. "Sorry to disturb you, Jordan. But there are two detectives here. I told them that you were busy working, but they really want to talk to you."

Jordan realized they were trying to help. But their timing was awful. He was welding a few of the pieces to the base of the sculpture. He removed his glasses, gloves and mask.

"Thank you, Lydia. Please, ask them to come in."

Lydia returned with two detectives who introduced themselves as Detectives Halstead and Gomez.

"We found some footage of the person, who we believe to be the suspect, leaving your studio at the time of the incident." Detective Gomez held up a tablet.

"That's fantastic." Jordan was relieved. He stood beside the man so he could see the video. "Where'd you get it? I don't have any cameras on the building. Though, after this incident, it's clear that I should."

Detective Halstead produced a notebook from his pocket. "It came from the jewelry store on the other side of the alley. Their camera is positioned to protect their space, so I warn you, the footage is grainy."

"We never got a clear picture of the suspect's face," Detective Gomez added. "But perhaps you'll recognize something about the suspect. His clothing, or perhaps the way he walks."

"No one wants to catch this wanker more than

I do, I assure you, Detectives. I'll do whatever I can to help."

Detective Gomez played the snowy video on his phone. He zoomed in on the suspect's face as much as he could. But the more he expanded the screen, the grainier the footage became.

"I'm sorry, I can't tell anything from this." Jordan sighed. It could've been his own mother and he wouldn't have been able to recognize her from that low-quality video.

"See those shoes?" Detective Halstead pointed them out with his pen. "Back at the lab, the boys say this is a brand that's real popular with the kids. That plus the build and size of the suspect leads them to believe that this is a kid. Possibly a teenager."

"A kid did this?"

Jordan couldn't imagine why a kid would want to ruin his work. There were a few children, including teenagers, at the event that night. But they were with their families in the gallery. None of them had come to the studio.

Besides, why would any of them bother with petty nonsense like this?

Jordan fully expected the detectives to ask about the teenagers in attendance at the event. However, Detective Halstead launched into an altogether different line of questions.

"Your assistant tells me you work with…underprivileged teens." Detective Halstead said the phrase as if it were a euphemism for *unsavory characters*.

His partner's cheeks flamed and his eyes narrowed, but the man didn't say anything.

"You got beef with any of them?" Detective Halstead asked.

"With any of whom?" Jordan folded his arms and stared daggers at the man.

"With your underprivileged students," he said.

"No, I don't. Why would you assume it's one of them? Just because they come from a poorer part of town doesn't make them thieves." Jordan's face was hot and his nostrils flared.

This was exactly the kind of negative assumptions the kids he worked with had to deal with every day.

Bad behavior certainly wasn't limited to the "wrong" side of the tracks.

Jordan had been a rich kid all his life. He was well aware of the mischief and mayhem children from wealthy families were capable of. Yet, the detectives hadn't even asked about the kids that were there that night with their wealthy parents. The kind of people whose feathers the officers probably didn't want to ruffle.

"Besides, if we're going to look at teenagers, shouldn't we begin with the ones who were actually in attendance that night?" Jordan tried not to sound as irate as he felt.

"We were going to ask about them next," Detective Halstead said. "Made sense to start with the most likely suspects."

Jordan's hands clenched into fists at his sides. He tamped down the desire to punch the guy in the nose.

"My assistant Lydia will have a list of the attendees—including the handful of kids under twenty who were here that night." Jordan directed his comments at Detective Gomez, ignoring Detective Halstead. "So if there isn't anything else, I have a lot more welding to do before I call it a night."

"No, that'll be all for now. But if you do think of anything that might be of help to us, we'd appreciate any information you can give us." Detective Halstead slid his notebook back into his pocket.

Jordan was on his way back to the table where he was working, when a thought occurred to him. He turned back to the detectives.

"You didn't ask about my assistant Marcus? Nor did you request a list of the students that've worked in my studio in the past year. Does that mean you've already gathered that information?"

Detective Gomez frowned, his eyes lowered. He opened his mouth to say something, but Detective Halstead, obviously the lead detective, cut him off.

"Thank you for your cooperation, Mr. Jace. We'll keep you up to date on any new developments in the case. You enjoy your day."

After the detectives left, Jordan went back to work, stewing over the officers' assumption that his students were the likely vandals. Especially when there was a tidy pool of suspects in house the night of the event.

Though, Jordan couldn't imagine why any of them would want to destroy his sculpture, either.

On Jordan's next break, he took out his phone and called Sasha. He updated her on the latest developments in the case. Then he recounted his encounter with the officers.

"Sadly, that kind of thinking isn't uncommon," Sasha lamented. "I'm sure none of them are involved. But do you have any reason to believe that any of the Prescott George kids would be involved?"

"I can't imagine why anyone would do this." Jordan shook his head. "But, for now, I'll allow the good detectives to worry about it. My only concern is what you'll be wearing for dinner at my place this evening."

"If the past is any indication, not much." Sasha giggled.

Jordan grinned, remembering the last few nights they spent together. He could barely wait until she was inside the door before he had her naked and in his bed.

"I promise not to strip you of your clothing until after dinner this time."

"In that case, I'll wear something nice." The

sound of Sasha's laughter made Jordan's heart dance.

He wasn't sure what this was between them, but it was different from any involvement he'd had before.

More than sex. More than friendship. It was something truly special because she was someone truly special. Still, Jordan wasn't prepared to label it.

Why ruin what they had by trying to categorize it?

Seeing or talking to Sasha was the highlight of his day. Having someone he cared so deeply for, whom he could talk to about just about anything, brought him a sense of peace he hadn't known in so long.

So why couldn't he shake the uneasiness he felt about allowing someone else to become so central to his happiness?

"Hello, love."

Sasha never grew tired of the joy in Jordan's eyes when she arrived at his house at the end of their long workdays.

He gave her a quick kiss, took her overnight bag and put it in the bedroom.

Sasha inhaled the fragrant bouquets of red and white roses on the entry hall console table.

Jordan had them delivered each morning, before

she left for work. Another arrangement of fresh flowers was always at the center of the table on the terrace where they typically dined each evening.

Jordan would pick something out on his way home from the gallery. It was a sweet gesture, and she was delighted by the daily surprise.

"The flowers are gorgeous, Jordan." She made her way onto the terrace and inhaled the impressive presentation of hydrangeas, tulips and roses in red, white and hot pink. The scent was heavenly.

She enjoyed the lavish gift of daily fresh flowers, but felt guilty that he was spending so much on her. Jordan insisted that if they weren't restricted to dining in each evening, he'd spend much more on a night out.

Sasha returned to the kitchen, following the savory scent.

Jordan had wanted to go out to dinner every night, rather than either of them cooking at the end of a long workday. But Sasha didn't think it wise for them to be seen out eating together every night.

His compromise had been to have his personal chef come in each afternoon and make them a romantic meal.

One of the many ways he'd been spoiling her.

"Mmm. Dinner smells divine. What's on the menu tonight?"

"Leek-and-potato galettes and a pear salad. You're going to love them." Jordan joined her in the kitchen, wrapping his arms around her and nuzzling her neck. He kissed her again, sending a jolt of electricity down her spine, igniting sparks in every erogenous zone in her body. Her knees trembled, her nipples beaded and there was a steady pulse between her thighs.

Sasha pushed him away, laughing. "After dinner, remember?"

"A promise is a promise," he conceded with a groan.

He opened a bottle of the German Riesling she'd fallen in love with during their time together on the yacht. He poured her a glass and one for himself, taking the bottle with them to the table.

Sasha forced a smile as she sipped her wine, his words striking her with sadness.

*A promise is a promise.*

She couldn't remember being happier with anyone than she'd been in the moments she'd spent with Jordan Jace, from the very night they met. Yet, he'd been clear from the beginning that he wasn't interested in a long-term relationship. He'd given no indication that he'd changed his mind.

So how long would it be before Jordan kept his promise and walked away, leaving her with a broken heart?

After their delicious meal, she rinsed their dishes and loaded them into the dishwasher. Then she wrapped up the leftovers for their lunches the next day. It was the only way she could ensure that Jordan would take the time to eat.

The sculpture he was working on in memory of his sister was nearly complete. But he and Marcus were working on several smaller sculptures simultaneously. Many of them, Jordan had said, were inspired by Sasha.

He'd teasingly called her his muse. She was flattered, but how many muses had gone before her? And when her muse pixie dust wore off, would Jordan be ready to move on?

A knot twisted in her gut whenever she thought of this ending. Jordan was no closer to committing to a relationship, yet each day she grew fonder of him.

In the quiet moments when she contemplated where their relationship was going, the thought of it ending made her ill.

Yet, it was inevitable.

Jordan Jace didn't do relationships.

Eventually he would walk away, just as he had with every other woman with whom he'd been connected.

It was an eventuality she needed to prepare herself for. Right now, they were working together closely on revamping and strengthening his brand. But what happened once her work with him was done?

Sasha frowned, chewing on her lower lip.

"Darling, what's wrong?" Jordan approached her.

"Nothing." She quickly forced a smile. "How

could there be? I just had an amazing meal with the most amazing man. What more could I want?"

"I'm glad you asked." A wide grin animated Jordan's handsome face. He reached for her hand and led her to the bedroom. But he bypassed the bed and took her to the bathroom.

"Oh my goodness." Sasha covered her open mouth, stunned. The bathroom smelled of fragrant roses and the large spa tub was filled with milky water and rose petals. A chilled bottle of champagne, a dish of strawberries, candles and soft music completed the scene. "You made me a rose milk bath? This is incredible. Thank you." She hugged and kissed him.

"I know it isn't the same as going to a spa, but I hope you enjoy it." He smiled sheepishly. "I actually made this with my own hands." He held them up. "Let me know what you think."

"There is one important ingredient missing." She leaned over and peered into the milky water.

"What did I forget?" He frowned.

Sasha put her arms around his waist and stared up into his handsome face. "You."

He kissed her. Took his time undressing her. Then he helped her into the tub where he joined her. They sipped champagne and listened to soft, romantic R & B from some of her favorite artists he'd compiled on a playlist.

"You realize you just made me the modern equivalent of a mix tape." She leaned back against his chest, enjoying the warm, soothing, fragrant water. "You don't make a girl a mix tape unless you're serious."

Jordan chuckled, the sound vibrating against her back. He kissed her neck. "Yeah, I guess I did. It's the least I can do. You inspire me, Sasha. I've never been with anyone quite like you."

A great compliment, but he hadn't been inspired to commit to their relationship. And she'd happily give up the fresh flowers, chef-made meals, expensive champagne and rose milk bubble baths in exchange for the thing she wanted the most. For Jordan to say the words she wanted to hear.

That he felt as deeply for her as she felt for him.

She was falling in love with Jordan Jace, with no expectations that he might one day feel the same.

After their bath, Jordan took her to his bedroom. The entire room glowed with warm candlelight. The glittering San Diego skyline in the distance only made the scene more romantic.

Jordan took his time worshipping her body with a trail of delicate kisses that left her skin tingling in their wake. And his exquisite tongue ravished her most intimate parts, leaving her nipples throbbing and the most delicious ache between her slick thighs.

When they'd made love it was fiery and passionate. Yet, there was a tenderness and intimacy that felt new for them. Something deeper.

Something that felt a lot like love.

# Chapter 12

Jordan awakened early on a Saturday morning to work in his home studio. He sat at the old drafting table his grandfather had given him when he first discovered Jordan showed real promise as an artist.

He'd held on to the desk all these years. It was his way of holding on to his grandfather who—like his twin sister—had always believed in and encouraged him.

Jordan stared at a series of sketches he'd drawn of Sasha sleeping. When he awoke before she did, he often caught himself watching her sleep. Wondering what she was thinking.

The kind of thing lovesick fools did. Not that he

was in love. But he did *really* like Sasha. Enough that he'd made a habit of waking up to her gorgeous face every morning.

It was unlike him. Gossip reporters often made unflattering exaggerations about how quickly he shed romantic interests. However, he couldn't deny that there was a kernel of truth to those articles.

Long-term relationships weren't his thing.

It was usually a stretch to call them relationships at all. Flings would be more accurate. Not everyone approved of his lifestyle. Least of all his parents. Regardless, he'd been content with a revolving door of women to feed his creative muse.

But with Sasha, things were different. As an artist, he was inspired by her. But she wasn't just his muse. She was a friend. A confidante. And he could say with great certainty that he was a better person since Sasha Charles had come into his life.

She was a remarkable woman. The moment she entered a room, she filled it with light and energy. And even on his darkest days, she instantly brightened his mood. Brought him out of the melancholy that sometimes settled over him. Made him feel worthy of her affection.

He dragged his fingers through his hair, disturbed by that thought. To the world he seemed confident, maybe even cocky. He walked in a room as if he owned it. Yet, there was an ever-present darkness inside of him.

Guilt. Uncertainty. Pain. Survivor's guilt.

They'd been part of his life since the day he'd lost his twin sister on that beach in Italy.

The clubs, parties and parade of women were meant to plug the hole that allowed that darkness to seep out. Instead, they'd simply been a mask for the pain he felt. But with Sasha, a little more of that cloud lifted. As if the pain of that tragic day, nearly twenty years ago, had started to heal.

Maybe that was why he felt more creative now, inspiration coming to him more easily. He had more project ideas than he could possibly hope to execute.

If he was the type of bloke who settled down, he'd be fortunate to do so with someone as incredible as Sasha Charles.

But variety was the spice of life. For Jordan, nothing stayed the same for long. His cars, his home, the way he wore his hair. The women on his arm. Change gave him a new perspective. Without that shift, life would be stale and repetitive.

As much as he cared for and wanted Sasha, he knew himself. And people didn't change. Not at their core. So as impossible as it seemed, he knew that one day things would change between them. What they shared would no longer be enough.

There was a gentle tap at the door. "Jordan, do you mind if I come in?"

Sasha's sleep-filled eyes were partially closed. She wore the pink La Perla baby-doll nightgown he'd purchased for her. The brown peaks visible beneath the sheer silk georgette created tension in his shaft.

"Did I wake you, love? If I did, I'm sorry. I couldn't sleep, so I got up to do some preliminary sketches. Here, take a look."

"These are all of me?" She sat on his knee and surveyed the pencil sketches.

He pulled her back against his bare chest and kissed her neck. "I told you, darling, you inspire me. You inspire my work. You've prompted me to make new connections. I even seem to be getting along with my dad better these days, thanks to you."

He slipped the nightgown off her shoulder and kissed it. "I'm even considering a new opportunity."

"Oh?" She glanced over her shoulder at him.

"I've been invited to do a series of openings in Europe—France, Greece, Germany, Spain. I'd be gone for about six months."

"Oh." Same word, much different tone.

"That's not even the best part." He studied her face. "I want you to come with me, Sasha."

She stood, turning to face him. "Jordan, I can't leave my job for six months."

"Make it a working trip. There's no reason you can't work on other client projects, like you did on the yacht."

"That was for seven days. You're talking about half a year. I can't justify that."

"Then take a leave of absence." He pulled her onto his lap again. "C'mon, love, it'll be fun knocking about Europe together."

"You don't get it, do you?" Sasha stood again. This time she walked around the table so she was facing him. "I can't just take off with you like that. How do I know that you'll still even be interested in me in six months or even two? That certainly isn't your usual MO." Her voice was strained and her expression was taut.

"I thought you'd be excited to go to Europe. You said you always wanted to go. That's why the opportunity seemed perfect for us."

The corner of Sasha's eyes were suddenly damp. "That's just it, Jordan. There really is no *us*, is there? I mean, don't get me wrong, I care very much for you. And being with you is like this crazy, exciting fairy tale where I never know what's going to happen next. It's fun, and it's exciting. But, Jordan, underneath it all, I'm still that organized planner. The girl who needs order in her life."

She sat in a chair on the opposite side of the room, her arms wrapped around herself. "I'm not a college coed, Jordan. I'm ready to begin the next phase of my life. I thought I could be okay with going with the flow. Living your life of spontaneity. But I need to ask you a question, and I need you to promise me that you're going to tell me the absolute truth."

Jordan blew out a long breath. He joined her in the arrangement of seats and nodded, bracing himself for the train that he could already feel rumbling down the tracks.

"Shoot. Ask me anything you'd like. I promise to tell you the truth. No matter what."

Sasha stared for a moment at her hands, folded in her lap before looking up at him. "Being with you has been amazing. I wouldn't trade what we've shared for anything in the world. But I need to know where you see this going?"

Jordan heaved a sigh and sat back against the chair.

It was the beginning of the end.

Even as Sasha formed the words in her head, she wished she was the type of girl who didn't need to ask.

She'd attributed her need for an answer to the phase of her life she now found herself in. But the truth was she'd never been the kind of person who'd enjoyed doing things by the seat of her pants.

"I don't know, Sasha. This is all really new for me, too. I'm not typically the kind of bloke who scripts out his entire life on Saturday morning."

A direct knock on her unfailing habit of doing just so, surrounded by her collection of markers, productivity stickers and washi tape.

He was amused. She wasn't.

"This isn't funny, Jordan. You're asking me to drop everything and go to Europe with you for six months. I don't think I'm being unreasonable here." She stood and paced again.

"Maybe not. But you are being predictable and—"

"Boring?" She turned back to look at him, her arms folded.

"No." He scrubbed a hand down his face. "But you are being quite rigid. I know you love your to-do lists and plotting everything out in your trusty planner, but in my experience, that doesn't leave much room for spontaneity or the freedom to experiment. I'm an artist, Sasha. I have to have those things in order to be creative. Without them, I'm nothing."

"You're right. I know I can be a little crazy with my need for order and lists. And I love that you've shown me how great life can be when it isn't all mapped out. That it's okay to take a detour off the path. But, Jordan, for me, spontaneity is ice cream with sprinkles on top. I can't live on a steady diet of ice cream. I need substance. And for me, that means knowing what comes next."

"I'm sorry, Sasha. But I won't make promises I may not be able to keep. I care about you too much to mislead you." He sat back in his chair and rubbed his palms on his pajama pants. His eyes didn't meet hers. "I honestly don't know where this goes. And I won't make empty promises."

Her heart crumpled and her knees were suddenly too weak to bear her weight. She slid into the chair again.

She'd been willing to try things his way. And it'd been wonderful. But he was asking her to drop everything and put her life and career on hold for six months. All without giving her any kind of commitment or assurance.

For him, she wanted to be that girl. But she couldn't. She needed to know how he felt about her.

"I'm trying really hard here, Sasha. We're practically living together, and I assure you, that is not the norm for me. The flowers, the dinners, the gifts... they're all tokens of my deep affection for you."

"And I appreciate it." Sasha squeezed his hand, finally raising her eyes to his. "But remember what I told you that first night...you don't need to try so hard. Because while I enjoy being here in your beautiful home on the bay in Coronado, driving in fancy cars and wearing expensive lingerie... I don't *need* any of it. And none of those things are the reason I want to be with you."

"And why do you want to be with me, love?" He winced, his question a pained whisper. As if he were afraid of hearing her response.

"Because you're brilliant. And you're funny. You always make me laugh, regardless of what's going on in my world. You're a smart-ass who challenges me. But you're also incredibly thoughtful. You made me step out of my comfort zone and try new things. And you've allowed me to do the same for you." She wiped tears from the corners of her eyes.

"*That's* why I'm with you, Jordan. That's why I want you. It's why I think of you all the time. About what it would be like to build a future with you."

His eyes widened, as if he'd seen the ghost of Monogamy Future and he didn't like what he'd seen.

He stood and paced, his hands on his hips. "Why can't things just be as they are, without labels or expectations? If we're meant to have a future together, it'll reveal itself along the way."

Her eyes stung with tears. She stood, too. "This experiment…perhaps it was a mistake." Tears streamed down her cheeks. She wiped angrily at them.

"Are you saying that—"

"Right now, I don't know what I'm saying other than… I can't go to Europe with you. And I need to go home to my own apartment. Clear my head a bit."

Sasha turned and left without saying goodbye. She went to the bedroom, packed her bag and left the La Perla gown on the bed.

Deep down, she wanted Jordan to come after her. To beg her to stay. But he hadn't. And that was everything she needed to know.

Jordan didn't care enough to fight for her.

## Chapter 13

Jordan had been frustrated and antsy since Sasha had left. He'd been terrified of saying the thing that would make her stay, but he was furious with himself for letting her go.

He wasn't sure if he wanted a future with Sasha, but he knew that if she walked away from him, his life would never be the same. She'd only been gone an hour and already it felt as if things were falling apart.

Everything he'd tried to draw was utter garbage. As if his muse had taken the creativity she'd inspired in him, tucked it in her pocket and walked right out of the front door.

He left his home studio, no longer able to stare at the sketches of Sasha.

Jordan needed to do something with his hands. He drove to the studio to work alone on the sculpture for his sister. The piece was in the finishing stage. It was the kind of work he often handed off to Marcus. But on this piece, he wanted every surface to be finished by his own hand.

Jordan shook a can of spray paint. It slipped from his hand and rolled beneath one of the tables. He dropped down on all fours and peeked underneath. A metal item sparkled in the light and caught his eye.

He retrieved the item, climbed to his feet and examined it under the light. It was a girl's charm bracelet. One he'd seen before.

Jordan closely examined the charms. Ballet shoes. A tennis racket. A moon. Stars.

*Headphones.*

Now he remembered where he'd seen that charm before. It belonged to Chris Marland's daughter, Jojo. She'd been at the event that night and she wasn't thrilled that her day with her father had been spent with him mostly handling club business.

Jordan took out his mobile and rang Sasha before he even realized it. She'd become the first person he rang to share his news, be it good or bad.

She was furious with him and on the verge of

walking away. He should let her alone. End the call and ring Chris to ask him to meet with him.

But he let it ring.

He needed to hear her voice. To know she was okay.

Sasha didn't answer. When the call rolled over to voice mail, he wanted to tell her all the things she wanted to hear. Anything to make her come back to him.

But he promised her he wouldn't lie. Even if it meant that one or both of them would be hurt.

"Hey, Sasha, it's me. I may have discovered who the vandal and break-in artist is. If you get this message within the next hour, meet me over at Prescott George HQ." He paused, not knowing what else to say. "Thanks, love."

He snapped a few photos of the bracelet and sent them to Sasha. He wouldn't notify the detectives just yet. He'd give Chris the opportunity to resolve the matter internally. Save him and the club the embarrassment of handling this publicly.

Next, he called Chris and asked the man to meet him straightaway. He deserved to learn of Jordan's discovery face-to-face.

Jordan paced the floor of his office at Prescott George. Chris Marland wouldn't be happy when he learned what he discovered.

Still, if anyone had the right to be angry it was

him. The bracelet proved Chris's daughter had been in his studio—where she had no business. The girl had caused him valuable time and money and vandalized the most important piece he'd ever created.

He blew out a long, steady breath and thought of what Sasha would say. She'd remind him that Jojo was just a kid and that she was having a tough time dealing with her parents' divorce. And so was Chris.

"Did you really need to drag me down here?" Chris dropped into a chair in Jordan's office, his brows furrowed. "This is interfering with my time with the kids. The last thing I need is another conversation with my ex today."

Jordan gritted his teeth. He sat on his desk in front of Chris and quickly counted to ten in his head.

"I wouldn't have brought you down here on a Saturday if it wasn't absolutely essential, I assure you. My day has already gone pear-shaped, and this isn't making it any better." Jordan strained as much of the irritation from his tone as he could.

"So, spit it out. What is it?"

Jordan pulled the bracelet from his pocket and held it up. "I found this."

"Thank God. That's one of the things her mother was pitching holy hell about this morning. She blamed me because apparently Jojo lost it when she was with me. Guess she was right about that part at least." Chris examined the individual charms and the chain. "Damn, it's broken. I'll have to get it repaired. Where'd you find it? Did she lose it the night of the event at your gallery?"

"Yes, in fact, she did." Jordan folded his arms. "I found it underneath one of the worktables in my studio."

"You mean the gallery. Jojo wasn't in your studio." Chris narrowed his gaze.

"I didn't think she had been either, until I saw that chain under the table."

"Wait, are you accusing Jojo of what I think you are?" Chris glared at Jordan. His nostrils flared as he lifted his chin.

"No need to get your knickers in a twist, mate. I take no pleasure in accusing your daughter of this. But the bracelet proves she was there, and she seemed angry enough at you and the world to make trouble that night. Not to mention, I distinctly remember there being a period when you couldn't locate her."

Chris was furious, completely blind where his daughter was concerned.

"Look, I'm not blaming you personally for what she did. I'm simply informing you of what I found. I would think you should thank me."

"Thank you?" Chris shot to his feet. "For what? For falsely accusing my daughter?"

"You've seriously lost the plot, haven't you? Did

you not just hear what I said? I found your daughter's bracelet under the table in my studio where she ought not have been. She's been caught bang to rights." Jordan was losing his patience.

Was the man a complete imbecile?

"This is about you trying to protect one of those kids you work with or maybe your studio assistant, isn't it? Well you're not going to pin this on my little girl. Trespassing in your studio? Destroying a sculpture? The vandal also broke in here at headquarters. Jojo's a good girl. She isn't even capable of doing the things you've accused her of."

"If I had a penny for every naïve father who has ever thought that about his little girl, I'd have enough to purchase my own professional basketball team with plenty to spare."

"Jojo's only thirteen. She's never been in trouble a day in her life. This isn't about her at all. This is about you shifting the blame."

Jordan stood, too. They were nearly standing nose to nose. "I take back what I said about not blaming you personally. You're completely clueless. Your little girl has you wrapped around her little pinkie."

"You're a liar." Chris shoved a finger in Jordan's face. "Maybe you trashed your own sculpture."

"Now you sound like a complete nutter." Jordan's face and neck were hot. He gritted his teeth, trying to keep some semblance of calm. "Do you have any idea how much money and work the damage to that piece caused me? Why on earth would I put myself through that?"

"To deflect blame from yourself and throw us off the trail after the residue of that powder you use was found in the break-in here."

"You honestly believe me capable of such subterfuge?"

"Why not? You lied the other day about staying here to work on community outreach when you were really here to hook up with that little consultant of yours who's always hanging around."

"What are you talking about?" Jordan glared at the man. His jaw tensed.

"I left my phone and I had to come back here. I heard you two going at it in the library. Seriously, are you fifteen? Don't you have a house and a business where you can take your little girlfriend and screw her?"

"I suggest you shut your trap and get the hell out of my office before I take this evidence to the two detectives who showed up at my studio the other day eager for a new lead." He wanted to punch the tosser in his face. Perhaps rearrange a few of his teeth.

"If you even think of accusing my daughter of this, I'll make sure everyone knows you're sleeping with your consultant. And I'll be sure to mention that it was your mother who arranged the entire affair."

"You wouldn't dare."

"Try me." Chris shoved over a chair and rushed out of the office, nearly bowling over Sasha who'd just arrived. He turned back to Jordan and stared at him pointedly.

"What on earth got into him?" She reached to sit the chair upright, but Jordan waved her off and did it himself.

"Have a seat." He indicated the sofa. "Please."

She sat on the leather sofa in her flowing poet's blouse, a pair of jean shorts and sneakers.

Jordan sat beside her, leaving space between them. He tried his best to ignore her bare thighs, close enough to touch.

"What is it, Jordan? Why was Chris Marland so upset?"

He swallowed hard, reluctant to meet her gaze. "The bracelet I sent you pictures of…it belongs to Jojo Marland. I found it under the table in my studio."

"Jojo's the kid who broke into your studio and damaged the sculpture?" Her eyes widened.

"I'm afraid so."

"Then why is her father upset with you? What am I missing?"

"First, he's dead from the neck up where any

wrongdoing by his precious little daughter is concerned."

"He didn't believe you? Not even after you told him where you found the bracelet?"

"He thinks I planted it."

"Why on earth would you do that?" She turned her body to him, her eyes widening in disbelief.

Jordan groaned, wishing he could spare her the dirty details of Chris's threat. But she needed a heads-up, in case he followed through on his threat.

"While investigating the break-in here, they found residue of a chemical I use to clean metal. Vaughn had to question me, but he quickly moved on from the idea. Chris is trying to make it seem that I trashed the sculpture myself in order to throw suspicion off me. Or that maybe I'm framing Jojo to protect Marcus or one of my students."

"That's insane. I know he loves his little girl. But she's a teenage girl. They're capable of just about anything. I was one. I should know."

"That isn't the worst bit." A knot tightened in his gut as he anticipated her reaction. "The day you and I were here in the library… Chris returned to retrieve his phone and he heard us. If I tell the police about Jojo, he's threatening to tell the world about you and me."

# Chapter 14

"Oh my God." Sasha covered her mouth, her eyes pressed shut. She was sure she was hyperventilating and it felt like she was going to throw up. "This cannot be happening. If this gets out, my reputation will be ruined."

"I'm sure Chris is just flexing his muscles to get me to back off, but I wanted you to be aware of his threat, just in case."

Sasha paced the floor, barely listening to anything Jordan said after "he's threatening to tell the world about you and me."

"No one would ever take me seriously again.

And I'd never be able to work in San Diego again. Your mother would see to that."

"Let me worry about my parents." He sighed. "But if we play our cards right, it won't ever come to that."

"How do you know Chris won't run with this story just to be vindictive? Or to discredit you as a preemptive strike." She wrapped her arms around herself, trying to stop the shuddering.

A few hours ago, she would've given anything to have Jordan hold her in his arms and tell her everything would be okay. And now she wished she could go back to when she first met Eva Jace and tell her *hell no*. She wasn't interested in working with her son.

"He wouldn't. Chris is the president of the chapter. We're having enough problems as it is. He wouldn't want to compound them."

"It's his daughter, Jordan. He'd do anything to protect her. Blood above club. It's what you do for the people you love." Sasha sank onto the sofa again, her hands shaking. "I'm so screwed. I'm going to lose everything I've worked for my entire career. That's what I get for breaking the rules. After all, that's why they're there. To prevent disasters like this."

"I'm so sorry, love. I feel like a heel. This is all my fault." He squeezed her hand. "I'm going to fix this, Sasha. I promise you, I will do whatever it takes."

She didn't look up at him or acknowledge his promise. Why should she? He hadn't been willing to put his heart on the line for her. He hadn't even gone after her when she'd left.

"This isn't your fault, Jordan, it's mine. You're just being who you've always been. I should've stayed with my plan." She stood, pulling her hand from his. "I showed poor judgment. Put my desires ahead of my obligations to my firm and my client. I won't make that mistake again. We need to get ahead of this."

"How?" He cringed, and she could tell he already knew what was coming.

"First, I can't be your consultant anymore. I'll assign else someone from our office. I'll just have to explain to your parents. They shouldn't be blindsided with this."

He stood, cupping her cheek. His voice little more than a whisper. "What about us?"

"There is no us." Tears stung her eyes and her entire body trembled slightly with the effort of holding back all of the hurt and pain that statement packed. "You can't commit, and I deserve nothing less. We're at a stalemate, Jordan. It's time to walk away."

He caught her hand and his touch set off a wave

of shivers inside her. She felt as if she were melting from the inside out.

"Please, don't make this any harder." She lifted onto her toes and gave him a quick kiss.

Before she could pull away, Jordan tugged her into his arms and kissed her. His tongue slipped between her parted lips and he wrapped his arms around her waist. He held her as if he had no intention of ever letting her go.

Sasha pressed the heel of her hands to his chest, disrupting their kiss. She stared into his eyes. Maybe she was only seeing what she so desperately wanted to see.

*Love.*

The same emotion she felt whenever she looked at him. But he couldn't say the words, and she wasn't a mind reader.

She wouldn't gamble her heart on a maybe.

"Goodbye, Jordan." She returned to her car as quickly as she could. Then she drove to the San Diego home of Jonathan and Eva Jace.

They deserved to hear the truth from her in person.


Jordan had been expecting a call from his parents, complete with a well-deserved tongue-lashing for banging the consultant they'd hired for him. But his mother had insisted on coming to his place to talk.

That meant she was steaming mad. Mad enough that she didn't want his father to hear what she was going to say to him.

He'd spent the two hours before his mother was due to arrive swimming laps in his pool, then showering.

Jordan opened the door and accepted his mother's kiss on the cheek, glad that she hadn't chosen to greet him with a cricket bat instead.

They sat on the terrace and he served her a cup of the Twinings Earl Grey jasmine tea that he kept on hand for her visits.

She sat down on the warm terrace and sipped her tea as she enjoyed the daytime view of the San Diego skyline.

His mother had been there nearly half an hour and she hadn't said a word about Sasha. He couldn't take it anymore.

"Look, Mother, I know Sasha rang you. So please, out with it already."

"You're wrong. She didn't ring. She came to see us because she wanted to look us in the face and apologize for letting us down and for letting you down."

"She came to you and Dad? When? Today?"

"Yesterday, right after she left you at the club. She rang from the car and asked if she could come over to talk with us." His mother put down her teacup. "She did her best to keep her chin up, but it was obvious Sasha was devastated by the entire affair."

"Chris hasn't been accepting my calls. I don't even know if he's bothered to ask his daughter how her bloody bracelet got into my studio. I'll try ringing him again today, now that he's had some time to cool down."

Jordan seethed, thinking of how devastated Sasha had been. She wouldn't take his calls, either.

"I won't allow Sasha to lose her job. Nor will I sit idly by while her reputation is ruined," he assured his mother.

"I love you, son, but you can be remarkably dim when it comes to affairs of the heart." His mother shook her head. "I'm not implying Sasha doesn't care about her career. Of course, she does. But what I saw was a broken heart because the man that she loves doesn't love her back."

Jordan swallowed hard. "She told you that?"

"She didn't need to, son. It was obvious to anyone who wished to see it."

Jordan sipped from his cup of tea, absorbing his mother's words and taking inventory of his own feelings for Sasha. Something he'd done again and again in recent weeks.

"I care about her very much. I haven't stopped thinking about her since she left here yesterday morning. I want to be with her, Mum. I do. But I won't hurt her by promising her something I'm simply not capable of."

"Darling, what makes you think yourself incapable of loving and being loved?" She squeezed his hand.

"History, Mother. My romantic entanglements have a shorter life expectancy than the common housefly. Or don't you keep up with the gossip blogs?"

A warm smile curled the edge of his mother's mouth. "Haven't gotten a single alert about your love life since we put Sasha on the case."

"True." He sipped his tea. "I suppose that is something."

"No, *she's* quite something. I knew from the moment I met her that you two would hit it off." She smiled slyly, quite proud of herself.

"You arranged this whole affair?"

"Let's just say I gave the cosmos a little help. Otherwise, I'll be dead and gone before I have any grandchildren to speak of." She chuckled softly. His mother was quiet for a moment, her bright eyes suddenly dimmed. "It'd be nice to have another daughter in the family, too."

She dotted her eyes with a tissue and sniffled. "You're not the only one who misses her, you know. Not a day goes by that I don't think about your sister."

Jordan pressed his eyes closed and shook his

head. "Then why do we never talk of her? As if she never existed?"

"We don't do that for us, son. We've always done it for you." She wiped away tears. "You've always carried around this huge sack of guilt over your sister's death. We were trying to protect you. But in doing so, it seems we've caused more harm than good. For that, I'm sorry."

They sat in silence, drinking their tea. Finally, she turned to him.

"Jordan, I know you feel badly about what happened to your sister, but you can't keep behaving as if you don't deserve love and happiness. Jeanette wouldn't have wanted that. She adored you, and she'd want you to be happy. Deep down you know that, but you're scared."

He turned away, studying the skyline. Fighting back the emotion that burned his eyes and his throat.

It'd been his fault. He was the one who'd wanted to swim out too far that fateful day. He called his sister a chicken when she hadn't wanted to do it.

Jeanette was pulled under by a wicked undertow. He'd dived under again and again, searching for her. Determined to find her or die trying. Finally, lifeguards had dragged him from the water, kicking and screaming because he refused to leave her alone out there. They recovered his sister's body the next day.

"What if I'm a dreadful partner? I don't want to ruin another life. Especially not Sasha's. She deserves someone who can truly love her. Not someone who's trying to figure it all out."

His mother squeezed his arm. "Talk to her, son. Tell her how you feel. She's a smart, capable woman. Give her the dignity of deciding for herself whether she's willing to take the risk."

"She is pretty special, isn't she? And she knows how to handle Dad. That's a definite plus."

They both laughed.

"A woman like that doesn't come along every day, son. So, if you love her, don't let her go. You'll always regret it."

He did love her.

And now that he'd had Sasha in his life, his world felt painfully empty without her.

# *Chapter 15*

Sasha had opted to work from home all week, just in case Christopher Marland decided to play his hand. The two partners at her firm that she'd apprised of her dilemma had been understanding.

They didn't want to lose her, nor did they want her reputation within the firm to be tainted unnecessarily. So they opted to keep the situation to themselves, only sharing the news with the other partners if it became necessary.

Sasha padded across the floor in her bare feet, glad that her work wear for the day consisted of a pair of gray yoga pants and a pink racer-back tank.

While she was officially off of Jordan's account,

it had yet to be assigned to someone else. So she kept a watchful eye over his social media accounts, ensuring that the scheduled posts went live at their appointed times.

She worked on a few of her other accounts and did a little laundry.

The doorman buzzed her and informed her that she had a visitor.

Jordan Jace.

After debating whether to change clothes, she decided against it. Sasha opened the door, determined that Jordan wouldn't have any effect on her. But when she was greeted by the handsome face and broad smile that haunted her dreams, her footing didn't feel as sure.

"Jordan, what are you doing here? You've never been here before."

It wasn't an accusation, it was simply a fact. But from the furrowing of his brows, he seemed to take it that way.

"You're right, and I'm sorry. About a lot of things." Jordan shoved his hands in his pockets and rocked back on his heels. "May I come in? I promise what I came to say won't take long."

Sasha nodded reluctantly and let him inside. She moved the lap desk with her computer and mouse off the couch.

"I'm working from home this week," she said by way of apology for the piles of papers on her couch.

She was glad there wasn't room on the couch for both of them. It would be better if she kept Jordan at a safe distance.

He sat in the chair she indicated, and she sat on the couch, her legs folded in a yoga easy pose.

Jordan looked uncomfortable or perhaps ill. Finally, he slid forward in his chair and swallowed hard.

"Sasha, I don't know what to say except… I need you. Please, don't walk away."

*The account. Of course.*

She tried to hide her disappointment that he'd only come to ask her to stay on his account.

"I know it'll be an adjustment at first, but it'll be fine. Whoever takes over the account is going to follow the same plan we discussed."

He looked puzzled at first, but then he shook his head. Jordan moved to sit on the table in front of her.

"No, you don't understand. I don't care about the account…well, I do…but that's not why I'm here."

He held her hand in both of his. "I'm here to tell you I'm sorry I was such a coward. That I was afraid of how you made me feel. I'm trying, rather badly, to tell you… I love you, Sasha."

"You…you love me?" Sasha blinked back the tears that stung her eyes. "Since when?"

He smiled, cradling her cheek. "From the moment you concocted that phony interpretation of my sculpture. We'd known each other less than five minutes, and it felt like we were old friends straight-away. I knew you were a woman who'd challenge me. And that you wouldn't let me take myself too seriously."

"You didn't." She couldn't help laughing, though her vision was blurred with tears.

"I did. I just didn't understand what I was feeling. But the moment I knew you were someone I should never let go of is when I learned you stuck up for me with my father—the man who was signing your checks. I thought, this woman is fearless and ride-or-die loyal."

Sasha smiled at the memories, moved by the sincerity of his words. Tears brimmed in her eyes and rolled down her cheeks.

Jordan frowned, wiping away the dampness on her face with his thumb. "Sorry I didn't tell you then, love. I wasn't ready, but I am now. I don't want to lose you, Sasha. Stay, please. My world isn't the same without you in it."

"I want to believe you, Jordan. I honestly do. But I couldn't bear it if you were only saying what you think I want to hear."

"Sweetheart, I promised I'd tell you the truth. That hasn't changed. I'm not saying what you want to hear, I'm telling you how I feel. I'm telling you what I was afraid to say before. I love you, Sasha Charles. And I want to be with you, and only you.

But I need to know how you feel about me, and if you still want to give this relationship a chance."

Her heart, impossibly full, expanded inside her chest. She couldn't form the words she needed to say, so she nodded, then pressed her lips to his.

"Yes, you love me? Or yes, you'll stay?" Jordan asked when he finally dragged his mouth from hers.

Sasha grinned, tears staining her cheeks. "Both."

Jordan heaved a sigh of relief. "There's one other thing you need to know… I'm totally new at this love thing. I know it won't always be easy, but I'm a fast learner. I'll do everything in my power to make you happy, Sasha." He kissed the palm of her hand. "Just be patient with me and stay by my side, and I swear, I will always be there for you, for better or worse. Because I want to wake up to you every single day for the rest of my life."

"Wait, are you saying that you want to—"

"Marry you? Yes. That's exactly what I'm saying. I finally found the woman I want to be with for the rest of my life."

"Oh my God. Jordan, are you sure about this? I mean, for a guy who's new at this love thing, you catch on pretty quick."

"Had a little help seeing the light." He squeezed her hand. "Apparently, the cosmos wasn't working fast enough."

"Then yes." Sasha's smile lit her brown eyes and

ignited a fire inside his chest. An undying flame that ushered warmth and light into the recesses of his heart, driving away the cold and darkness he'd held on to for so long. "I don't ever want to go back to life without you again."

Jordan pulled her into his arms and kissed her as tears slid down her cheeks.

The raging, jumble of emotions he felt for this woman were unmistakable.

It was pure, unadulterated love.

# *Epilogue*

Sasha lay out on the deck of the private sailboat, soaking up the warmth of the sun. She and Jordan were exhausted and in need of some quiet time alone.

The previous day had been marvelous. She and Jordan had spent the entire day with his parents and brothers; her best friend Miranda and her husband, Vaughn; Sasha's family; and several members of the local chapter of Prescott George.

They'd commemorated the life of Jordan's twin sister, Jeanette, with laughter and love during a festive, community dedication ceremony for his sculpture. The public art piece was a stunning tribute to

Jeanette, dedicated on the twentieth anniversary of the day they'd lost her.

It wasn't a sad occasion. The Jaces spent the day recounting heartwarming memories of the daughter and sister who'd touched them all. And thanks to the generosity of Jace Investments and the Prescott George San Diego Chapter, the sculpture had been installed at the future location of the Jeanette Jace public park.

Then in eight weeks, Jordan and Sasha would spend six months traveling to galleries in Britain, France, Greece, Spain and Germany with a large, curated collection of Jordan's work.

Sasha couldn't have been any prouder of him. And Jonathan, Eva and Jordan's brothers had been telling everyone they knew about Jordan's European art show.

"Hungry, love?" Jordan placed a tray on the table beside Sasha. His bare chest glistened with a sheen of sweat in the midday sun.

"Are we talking about another serving of you or the food?" Beneath the cover of her sunglasses, she scanned the tall, dark glass of sexiness she got to come home to at the end of every night.

The ridge beneath his swim shorts indicated that he was probably scanning her body, too. Most of it exposed in her tiny, white floral bikini.

"Let's start with the food and see where things

go." He winked. His generous smile still made her heart beat faster every time he flashed it at her.

"Fair enough. What are we having, handsome?"

Jordan had insisted on packing and preparing their lunch and dinner himself. He lifted the lid of the silver warmer with a flourish. "Steak, baked potatoes, salad and lemon meringue pie, milady."

"Everything looks fantastic." Sasha spread out her napkin. "My compliments to the chef."

Jordan nodded as he sat across from her. He poured two glasses of Brut Rose Ace of Spades Champagne and handed her one.

*"Fancy."* She sipped her Champagne. "What's the special occasion?"

Jordan didn't respond, but the sunlight sparkled off of something in the bottom of her glass.

Sasha gasped, tears burning her eyes as she got a closer look. She fished the ring out of the glass with her fork.

She recognized the huge, radiant-cut diamond engagement ring set in platinum. She'd admired it when she and Miranda were out shopping a couple of weeks earlier.

"Jordan, it's absolutely beautiful." She held the ring up. It glimmered in the sunlight. She reluctantly dropped the ring onto Jordan's open palm.

He made the temporary surrender of her gorgeous engagement ring well worth it when he kneeled to the ship's deck on one knee and asked Sasha to marry him.

She practically screamed that she would.

Jordan slipped the ring onto her finger and pulled her into his arms and kissed her.

Sasha would thank her friend later. Right now, her only concern was giving a very special thanks to the man she was going to marry. The man she couldn't wait to spend the rest of her life with.

Jordan pulled her onto her feet and kissed her. The sweet engagement kiss quickly turned into a heated, passionate affair that left them both breathless.

Sasha pulled away and headed below deck, with Jordan on her heels, and a trail of discarded swimwear left in their wake.

Lunch would definitely have to wait.

* * * * *

KIMANI™
ROMANCE

# COMING NEXT MONTH
## Available April 17, 2018

## #569 IT MUST BE LOVE
*The Chandler Legacy* • by Nicki Night

Jewel Chandler's list of boyfriend requirements is extensive—and Sterling Bishop doesn't meet any of them. Sure, the wealthy businessman is gorgeous, but he also has an ex-wife and a young daughter. When steamy days melt into desire-fueled nights, Jewel wonders if he's truly the one for her.

## #570 A SAN DIEGO ROMANCE
*Millionaire Moguls* • by Kianna Alexander

Christopher Marland, president of Millionaire Moguls of San Diego, is too busy for a personal life. When Eliza Ellicott arrives back in town, he knows no woman has ever compared. A broken heart gave Eliza the drive to succeed, and she's opened a new boutique. Can she trust him again?

## #571 RETURN TO ME
*The DuGrandpres of Charleston* • by Jacquelin Thomas

Austin DuGrandpre never had a relationship with his father. Determined that his son—put up for adoption without his knowledge—won't suffer the same fate, he tracks him to the home of Bree Collins. The all-consuming attraction is unexpected, but when Bree learns Austin's true motives she faces potential heartbreak.

## #572 WINNING HER HEART
*Bay Point Confessions* • by Harmony Evans

Celebrity chef Micah Langston's ambition keeps him successful and single. He plans to open a restaurant in his hometown—and that means checking out the competition. Jasmine Kennedy is falling for Micah until she discovers his new venture will ruin her grandmother's business. Has betrayal spoiled her appetite for love?

# Get 2 Free Books,
## *Plus* 2 Free Gifts—
### just for trying the *Reader Service!*

A tap on her shoulder startled Jewel. She turned around and was
swallowed up by Sterling's piercing hazel eyes.

"Can I join you?"

Jewel's pulse quickened. She wanted to say no. She couldn't
control the effect he had on her. Despite that, she said yes. Sterling
eased his fingers between hers and they swayed to the music
together. Jewel felt as if she were back in school. Sterling had
never been the object of her affection then, but she felt something
brewing now.

Jewel physically shook her head to shake off whatever that
feeling was. She stepped back, adding space between Sterling
and her, then moved in time with the lively beat. Sterling matched
her step for step and before long they were engrossed in a playful
battle, stirring up memories of old popular dances. Next, a song
came on from their senior year. A certain dance was known to
accompany the rhythm. Jewel and Sterling joined the rest of those
on the floor, moving along with the crowd in unison. They danced,
laughed and danced more. Other songs began and ended and the
two were still dancing some time later. Dominique and Harper had
found partners, too, and were no longer beside Jewel and Sterling.

Sweat was beginning to trickle down the center of Jewel's back. Her body had warmed from all the movement.

"Whew! I need a break." Jewel panted, threw her head back and laughed. She hadn't danced that hard in years. She felt free. "That was fun."

"Let's get a drink." Taking her by the hand, Sterling led her off the dance floor and headed to the bar. He asked for two waters and handed one to Jewel. "Want to get some air?"

"Sure." Jewel took the ice-cold water Sterling had just handed to her. She moaned after a long sip. "I needed this."

Sterling took her hand again and led them to the terrace. Jewel was hyperaware of his touch as they snaked through the crowd, but didn't pull away. She liked the way his strong masculine hand felt wrapped around hers.

Once they hit the terrace, the cool air against her warm sweat-moistened skin caused a slight shiver. They maneuvered past people gathered in groups of two or three until they reached the far end of the terrace, which was lit mostly by the silver light of the moon. Jewel placed her hand on the marble parapet and slowly swept her gaze over the sprawling greenery of the country club and what she could see of the rolling hills on the golf course. Closing her eyes, she breathed in the fresh air, exhaling as slowly as she inhaled.

Sterling stood beside her. "Perfect night, huh?"

"Yes. It's beautiful. If my mother were here she would scrutinize every crevice of this place." Jewel turned to face Sterling and chuckled. "She's so competitive."

"So you've gotten it honestly."

"What?" Her brows creased. "Me? No."

Sterling wagged his finger. "I remember you on the girls' lacrosse team. Unbeatable. Let's not forget the swim team," Sterling added. "Didn't you make all-county, and weren't you named the scholar-athlete of the year?"

Jewel blushed. She'd forgotten all of that. "Well. Yes, there's that."

The two laughed and then eased into a sultry silence. Jewel and Sterling studied each other for a moment. The moonlight sparkled in his eyes. Jewel looked away first, turning her attention back to the lush gardens.

*Don't miss IT MUST BE LOVE by Nicki Night, available May 2018 wherever Harlequin® Kimani Romance™ books and ebooks are sold.*

Want to give in to temptation with
steamy tales of irresistible desire?

Check out **Harlequin® Presents®**,
**Harlequin® Desire** and
**Harlequin® Kimani™ Romance** books!

## New books available every month!

## CONNECT WITH US AT:

Harlequin.com/Community

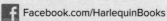 Facebook.com/HarlequinBooks

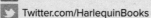 Twitter.com/HarlequinBooks

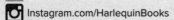 Instagram.com/HarlequinBooks

 Pinterest.com/HarlequinBooks

ReaderService.com

# HARLEQUIN®

**ROMANCE WHEN
YOU NEED IT**

PGENRE2017

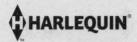